Sarah Helen Geyer

Copyright © 2021 Sarah Helen Geyer
All rights reserved
First Edition

PAGE PUBLISHING, INC.
Conneaut Lake, PA

First originally published by Page Publishing 2021

ISBN 978-1-6624-6023-4 (pbk)
ISBN 978-1-6624-6038-8 (hc)
ISBN 978-1-6624-6025-8 (digital)

Printed in the United States of America

This book has been written for those of you who love God and wish to learn more about him, those of you who are willing to search out a matter.

The exciting thing is, the more we learn, the more we find there is to learn about our Father, Jesus Christ, and the Holy Spirit.

I pray this book will be one that will provide you with much enjoyment and much information learned.

May our God bless you richly!

In loving memory of my brother, Mr. Larry D. Gill, without whom this book would not have been written.

There is for each of us a destiny to be lived out. We have destiny to be lived, but not alone. We were never intended to live alone. We were created as ones who need others around us. God has a need for fellowship with others, and we were created in the image of God. When we think of "in the image of God," we normally think of a physical image, but in reality, it is in every dimension known.

This is a stretch for some of us to go in this direction. We do not connect God with having the inner dimensions that we know we have.

The inner man that is present in our God is also present in us. We need others in our lives, as does our God. When God created man, he gave us the power to choose what kind of life we live or who we will follow while we are here on this earth. While giving us the freedom to choose, he also gave us the pleasure of choosing himself. The pleasures are mysteries to be revealed as we go through this life.

For then we find more within ourselves to give to others than we knew existed. When God begins to reveal to us the truth about ourselves, we find a whole new world opens up to us. Isn't this a mystery to be uncovered? The deep things inside us to be found out come as a great shock at times. It can be very scary if we allow it, but the things we find out about ourselves can be very exciting as well.

Now you must use your imagination in order to reveal these mysteries to yourself. It can be an opening to the most marvelous, exciting, overwhelming future if we allow it. The hint that you will reveal these secrets to yourself is a misquote. We do not teach ourselves secrets of life. This is a job for the Holy Spirit. He is constantly teaching us the importance of what may seem to be everyday occurrences, like a little bird that has been knocking on my patio door for the past five days.

Five days ago, I was visited by a pretty little bird that lives in a row of trees behind my home. He began to knock on my patio door with his beak. For five days now, he has been knocking on my door while I wonder what this is about. It is obvious God is using this little bird to tell me something, but I do not know what. I have come to the understanding of a mighty, wonderful truth about our God. As this little bird has extended his job of knocking on my door to over a week, I have extended my understanding of my Lord to looking deeper because this little bird allowed me to extend my understanding deeper and deeper. He allowed me the obvious option of extending my thoughts to a greater extent. For then I finally have realized the lesson of this little bird. Look deeper to the truths of our God. The riches of God are to be found in our everyday lives and experiences.

As I began to write this book, the meaning of it was not clear. Here comes the teaching concerning my little bird: go deeper. We must learn to go deeper in our everyday lives or we are destined to live quite mediocre lives, never reaching our level predestined by God.

It will take a reverse in our thinking to reverse how we see ourselves and others. We have become accustomed to looking at events and happenings in our world in a shallow manner. This is how we all see our world. How difficult it is to change our way of thinking. We must practice looking deeper to accomplish what is necessary to give us the best lives possible.

How did we begin to look at the surface only? It definitely takes little effort to live this way. Maybe this has something to do with the number of things that have come to our attention in the past couple of decades. Life is not an easy thing to deal with these days. We have more on our plates than ever before and less time to give it all our complete attention. With all the information that is readily available to us, we find we are stretched to the maximum. We have all heard the expression "too much information."

Usually when this is heard, it is said in a jokingly manner, but in reality, it is truth.

It may be a tall order to say we need to start looking at life in a deeper way than we are used to, but the rewards will be plentiful. The rewards will be not only plentiful but also well worth all the time invested.

God has planned a wonderful life for us both here on earth and when we go to heaven to live for an eternity with him, an eternity of wonderment and awe planned by a loving Father.

To begin to live this life of wonderment and awe, we must turn to the God who created us for his pleasure. If he created us for his pleasure, the knowledge we require to live out the life he has planned for us can only be attained through him.

This may seem like a tremendous goal to attain, but in reality, it is an easy one. If indeed this is what our heavenly Father wants for us, then we will discover all we have to do is ask. Those of you who have children certainly realize how proud you are when one of your children ask for advice. Our heavenly Father is no different when we go to him to ask for his help or advice. He longs for the opportunity to assist us with whatever we will allow.

How many times have I witnessed my child or grandchild going down the opposite path than the one I knew would lead to victory for them? The truth is, God cares for his children more than we do. That is not a put-down to us. This is only reality. We were made in the image of God, and if in his image, then why is it so difficult to understand his love and care for us? Grasping this truth can only deepen our understanding of God.

It is easy to assume that everyone is aware of the Trinity of God but not realistic. I wish to first go over the Godhead to make certain we all begin on the same page. There is God, the Father, Jesus Christ, God's only begotten Son, and the Holy Spirit, the Holy Spirit of God. Three separate but one in unity.

God, being the only living god. There are many gods in this world, but there is only one who is alive. Why would we want to worship a thing that is not alive, and if indeed your god is not a live being, what can he do for you? There are those who worship animals, but what can any animal do for you that warrants your worship? John 3:16 says God so loved the world that he gave his only begotten

Son that whosoever believes in Jesus Christ would not die but have everlasting life. Jesus chose to die on the cross to pay the price for sin so you and I would not have to.

The third part of the Godhead is the Holy Spirit of God, by which nothing can be accomplished without his aid. The Holy Spirit being the one that speaks to you, who calls you out of the world into his salvation and peace. The Holy Spirit being our teacher, our comforter, the one that draws us to Christ in the day of salvation. He is ever with us, never to leave us alone. It is written in 1 Corinthians 12:7, "But the manifestation of the Spirit is given to every man to profit withal"; 12:8, "For to one is given by the Spirit the word of wisdom; to another the word of knowledge by the same Spirit"; 12:9, "To another faith by the same Spirit; to another the gifts of healing by the same Spirit"; 12:10, "To another the working of miracles; to another prophecy; to another discerning of Spirits; to another divers kinds of tongues"; 12:11, "But all these worketh that one and self-same Spirit, dividing to every man severally as he will"; 12:18, "But now hath God set the members every one of them in the body, as it hath pleased him."

God has chosen us to be in his body of believers. He wishes that no one be left out. John 3:16 tells us that God so loved the world that he gave his only begotten Son that whosoever believeth on him should not perish but have ever lasting life. When Christ was crucified, he said that no one takes his life, but he gave his life of his own free will for you and me. What a love that has been bestowed upon us!

God still writes letters to us. We are made in the image of God. How do we accredit our propensity to want to speak to others, wanting to tell others the things we love about them, wanting to tell them we love them, wanting to tell them the things that will lead to their happiness? We have inherited the attributes of God. He said we were made in his image. This is where creation comes in. All those who fight against being associated with the living God do not realize the qualities that they most admire come from God himself. Think about what you could accomplish with the help of God. All you have to do is ask. God ever lives to have a relationship with us.

There is a pervasive assumption that has penetrated the Christian world for probably since the Bible was put together that needs to be exposed. This being that the Bible is too difficult to understand. What a hoax the devil has played on everyone who has believed that lie! I remember a time when I was thinking the same thing. I also remember asking God to help me understand what I felt I couldn't. It didn't take long until I noticed my difficulty had disappeared. Of course, the devil does not want you to read the Bible, but God does. His love for us requires our getting to know who he is. That is part of the excitement of beginning a relationship with God, getting to know him.

Upon getting to know who God is, you realize the wonder of God is that he is so massive we shall never come to know just who he is. We can begin to see different sides of him, but to know just who he is takes time. A lifetime with God means you have just begun. Now isn't that exciting?

The Bible says God is love, not that he loves but that he is love itself. You certainly do not have to wonder about your life with God. Love can never hurt you. Love can never let you down in any way. Love can do nothing but what is the very best for you. Isn't God awesome?

The beginning of this book looks at our beginning—not God's beginning, but ours. There was no beginning for God; he always was, and he will always be. You and I did have a beginning, and the first part of this book discusses this beginning. The beginning is always a good place to start.

When creation was taking place, the Word says Jesus Christ was present with God. The Word says without him was nothing made that was made. Along with Jesus being present, so was the Holy Spirit of God. The unity of God is always visible.

Creation has been attacked fiercely. If we will not accept creation, then we probably will not accept the creator. The reasonable action here would be to read what has been said about the creation process. With information in front of us, we can then decide for ourselves which way we will pursue. For the purpose of equipping the reader with reasonable information so you can decide for yourself, we offer you what the Bible says about creation.

The best way to know who Jesus is would be to have the living God telling us about his Son. Who better could relate the qualities of Jesus than his Father? Who better knows Jesus than his Father?

There are, no doubt, enough books printed to speak about Jesus for eons of years. Why would this woman, who is no one special, believe I can relate to you why Jesus is the most important man to be born of a woman?

The reason being I know him. He has brought me through some horrific things that I am sure I would not have come through without Jesus Christ. Throughout the worst days of my life, Jesus has allowed me to come to know him. When I thought my heart would break from pain, I found, because of the presence of Christ, there was strength I never felt before there to comfort me. This strength being the direct result of the presence of Christ Jesus.

You do not have to worry about asking Jesus to help. Jesus has sent his Holy Spirit to comfort, teach us all things, and bring all things to our remembrance, whatever it may take to lead us to the other side of pain. It is Jesus's pleasure to be there for us. This was the intention of Christ when he came to the earth to die on the cross for us. He chose to be born on earth of a woman and then die for our sins.

Jesus said, at that time, no one could take his life. He said he came to lay down his life for us. It was his decision to die for us.

You can study the Bible for years to learn a lot of what is in this book. Having let the spirit of God lead me, you will find the Scriptures that are in this book will give you a jump start on reading the Bible.

With my desire to introduce you to Jesus also comes his desire to let you introduce yourself to him. With our knowledge of Jesus comes an understanding of who we are. It gives Jesus pleasure to teach us who we are in him. There are so many mysteries about ourselves that are revealed when we begin to know who Christ really is. Who we really are is hid in God.

God says, in the Scriptures, we are made in the image of God. He said, "So God created man in his own image; in the image of God created he him: male and female created he them" (Genesis 1:27). Then in verse 28, it says, "And God blessed them."

In this book, you will find information about the Trinity of God, being the Father God, the Son, Jesus Christ, and the Holy Spirit. My hope is that you will find enough to make you know there is truth in this book that you cannot ignore. My prayer is that you will come away with a love and peace of God that will last you a lifetime.

I have also included a book of facts that will be of a tremendous help in the days to come. In this book, you will find that I have listed where to find each fact in the Bible. I have included this solely for your convenience.

God knows sometimes we are overwhelmed when opening the Bible. There is so much information in front of us we do not know where to begin. I believe this is the reason God has his people write books. He knows there is so much to learn that a book can be a good head start.

We are now living in the last days before Jesus returns to earth to take his children to heaven to live there with him. The time is short. The Bible tells us what the last days will be like, and the time line began when Israel became a nation again. In May of 1948, the Hebrew people regained the land that God had given them when he rescued them from Egyptian control.

God's Word said the information age would also be a sign. Who would argue against this being the information age?

The fact is, we will spend an eternity somewhere. I want everyone to understand what this means to us. We will spend eternity in either Heaven or a hell that was not created for man but was created for Satan and his angels. The restrictions are simple; it could not get any easier.

Either you believe in Jesus Christ as your Savior or you do not. What could be easier? The Bible says that Jesus sits at the right hand of God, ever making intercession for us. Everything Jesus did was for us.

"I will instruct thee and teach thee in the way which thou shalt go, I will guide thee with mine eye" (Psalm 32:8). This gives me much comfort. I like knowing if I get into trouble, there is someone who can help me. Life being what it is, let it be known that I have had to depend upon the Lord to help me. Thank God, for I have been in serious trouble. I am confident each of us could recall countless times when something occurred that was unexpected and instantly a miracle happened to rescue us.

This was our hero, Jesus Christ!

There happens to be a God who loves his children with a love that we cannot comprehend. His plans for us go beyond anything we could imagine.

He loves us so much that he talks to us in dreams, wanting us to understand his will for us. As we search the Scriptures, questions begin to arise. We find a lot of these questions can and will be answered as we read our Holy Bible. The Scriptures say:

> And ye shall eat in plenty and be satisfied, and praise the name of the Lord your God, that hath dealt wondrously with you; and my people shall never be ashamed. And ye shall know that I am in the midst of Israel, and that I am the Lord your God, and none else; and my people shall never be ashamed. And it shall come to pass afterward, that I will pour out my spirit upon all flesh; and your sons and your daughters shall prophecy, your old men shall dream dreams, your young men shall see visions. And also upon the servants and upon the handmaids, in those days will I pour out my spirit. And I will shew wonders in the heavens and in the earth, blood and fire and pillars of smoke. (Joel 2:26–30)

As this book is being written, it is understood that we are in the last days of this earth age.

> And it shall come to pass, that whosoever shall call on the name of the Lord shall be delivered; for in mount Zion and in Jerusalem shall be deliverance as the Lord hath said, and in the remnant whom the Lord shall call. (Joel 2:32)

God will indeed help us understand what we need to understand. He will not leave us unaware of something as important as our salvation. He has never left us alone; he will not start now. With a little reading and a little patience, we can come to understand more than we thought possible. Don't be fooled by the lie that you cannot understand the Word of God. It is a lie. It is my desire that as you read this book, some of your questions will be answered. There is a term that will appear many times, and it is "the church." Please understand, I'm not referring to a specific denomination or any specific church. I am using the term in general with the understanding that it is impossible for one to understand the differences of all denominations and all churches. The true meaning of "the church" is, in fact, the body of Jesus Christ. This is to say that every person who believes in Jesus and completely relies upon him for their salvation is a part of the body of Christ. This body is the "true church." When I use the term *the church*, it is not the "true church" I am referring to. Again, it is all the churches in general without regard to denominations or any specific church. When I use the term *the true church*, I am referring to everyone who genuinely relies and trusts in Jesus for his or her salvation making up the body of Christ.

There are those out there who claim to be Christians. It hurts the heart of God. The world has come to a universal agreement that whatever you decide to be truth is truth. If we keep going down this path that we have chosen, the truth will be presented to each of us, but at what cost?

Have you ever been caught in a nightmare that seemed that it would never end? When it first begins, it always seems like an unusually odd situation—nothing to worry about, just odd. As it progresses, it begins to show you the horror that is intended. You find yourself in a dream that wants to go on forever. This is, in reality, the kind of future Satan has planned for you.

The less we know about God and Jesus Christ, the easier it will be for us to be fooled into believing anything that is thrown at us. Since the Bible is such a huge book, it is difficult to know which book to turn to. My prayer and hope is that in this small book, the facts that are included will lead to a knowledge of Christ that you normally would spend years to learn.

I present this to you with love from our Father and Jesus Christ, our Savior. The time is short for all of us. Jesus is coming back very soon. We have a short time to learn of the one we will spend eternity with. The people of God are Christ's bride. He wants us to know him the way he knows us.

Part One—Acts
"In the Beginning"
Eternity Past

In the beginning God created the heaven
and the earth. (Genesis 1:1)

In this verse, God did not say when he did it, how he did it, or why he did it; the fact was stated God created the heaven and the earth. Man offers numerous theories to explain human presence on earth, ranging from the big bang theory to extraterrestrial life cloning man. I have heard the claim that man is nothing more than a three-dimensional image produced by holography. Believe it or not, this was a serious claim. The fact remains, God created the heavens and the earth. God offered no rebuttal to man's argument. God has no need to. He stated the fact, and the absence of rebuttal declares his power. Should God argue to convince man that God created man? This verse says it all and stands alone. In the beginning, God created the heaven and the earth (*period*). No explanations or arguments, this is the fact 1. If these were the only words ever to pass the lips of our Father, they would provide the information required to fill volumes of literary books. Verse 1 is not tied to verse 2 and is not a part of the first day of creation as taught by the church. Verse 1 is not tied to any verse in the account of creation in Genesis and is the only verse in Genesis dealing with the true creation. Verse 1 is the only verse in Genesis talking about creation? Imagine that! What the church teaches to be the account of creation has nothing to do with creation. What the church teaches to be the creation process in Genesis is, in fact, the destruction of the first earth age and the recreation of this earth age. The recreation process does not start at verse 1 but on day 2 in verse 6. The majority of events recorded in day 1 took place in eternity past. Day 1 starts with the commandment of God, "Let there be light." God is everlasting—meaning, as there is no end, there is no beginning. Days 2–6 simply reveal God's preparation for man on earth, revealing only the things God deemed necessary.

The age of our planet is not known, but scientists declare its age to be millions of years. The accepted teaching in the church is that the age of earth is just over six thousand years. This is calculated by adding from the Passion of Christ to Adam four thousand years (BC), to just over two thousand years in the year of our Lord (AD). Another teaching of the church calculates the earth to be just over thirteen thousand years. Because of the teaching of Peter that one day with God is a thousand years with man *(2 Peter 3:8)*, the seven days of creation are counted as a thousand years each added to the six thousand years man had inhabited earth in physical bodies. One needs only to walk into any museum and see the skeleton remains of dinosaurs to see that these teachings missed the mark on both accounts. Scientists adhering to the big bang theory envision man living in caves and being lunch prepared for dinosaurs, saying over time man evolved out of the water to Neanderthal man then to the sophisticated man he is today. Many in the church say that dinosaurs are not real but an attempt by man to discount the Word of God.

So many theories lead man to question where truth may be found. The truth is always found in God's Word. When one reads with understanding our Father's Word, you find God informed man of dinosaurs. Reference to the world of dinosaurs is found in the Old Testament as well as man in spiritual bodies before the creation of the earth in the New Testament. Man in a flesh body is quickly approaching the end of the earth age, but the earth had a prior earth age.

In the verse *Genesis 1:1*, we see that God did create the heavens and the earth. Perhaps we, as the church, owe the scientists an apology for disqualifying them because of this difference in opinion that has arisen because of the timing of the earth age.

The book of Job is believed, by some scholars, to be the oldest book in the Bible. If this is true, then the book of Job was penned before God used Moses to write Genesis through Deuteronomy. If the book of Job was read before Genesis, there would be no doubt in the reader's mind that God provided no details of creation or recreation in Genesis. It was not God's intention to describe the process by which God created or recreated this earth. God speaking to Job implied that he left out these details in Genesis.

> Gird up now thy loins like a man; for I will demand of thee, and answer thou me. Where wast thou when I laid the foundation of the earth? Declare if thou hast understanding. Who hath laid the measures thereof, if thou knowest or who hath stretched the line upon it? Whereupon are the foundations thereof fastened? Or who laid the corner stone thereof. (Job 38:3–6)

Just now, in your mind, did you say "Jesus" four times? While reading God's inquiry of Job, a couple of things become clear.

First God does pay attention to details. His questions are based on the details of his recreation of the earth starting at the beginning. The fact that God asked Job how the foundation was laid in detail is equivalent to God saying, "Look, Job, I didn't provide you the details, so if you know how I accomplished this with understanding, then tell me." Nowhere in Genesis can be found details of how the foundation of the earth was laid, nor can be found the account of measuring it. This is also true of how the foundation was fastened, set straight with the line and the placement of the cornerstone. It is all missing. Second, the first question our God asked Job was, "Job, when I laid the foundation to the earth, where were you?" Since God asked Job in detail while the real question asked was "Where were you?" the implication was that God did not supply the details. To answer God, Job would have had to witness recreation. In fact, the very next thing God told Job is that he did. "When the morning stars sang together, and all the sons of God shouted for joy?" (Job 38:7).

God clearly stated that all the "sons of God" were present when God recreated the earth. God's sons, so filled with joy, shouted. God's "morning stars" sang as the earth developed. This verse reveals there are two separate types of entities present. These two entities are represented by two separate terms. The first term is "the morning stars," and the second is "the sons of God." While reading our Father's Word and a term appears, if the meaning is not certain, we should first look for that term in other passages for the meaning. Our Father does not allow us to put a private interpretation on any part of *his Word*.

When God authored the Bible, he chose his Word very carefully to provide the specific meaning intended. For this reason, God chose the Hebrew and Greek languages to author the Bible. If we apply our own meaning to God's Word, we will never understand it. "Knowing this first, that no prophecy of the scripture is of any private interpretation" (2 Peter 1:20). Peter tells us the Bible was written not by man but by the inspiration of God. Each word spoken by our Father was chosen by God in its structure to provide a specific meaning. Terms found in one part of the Bible are repeated throughout our Father's Word. When God explains a term, we understand that meaning when the term appears again. This is another example of why using a Bible concordance is so valuable to the student of God's Word. It allows the student to look up a term and find every place in the Bible it is used, as well as providing the definition of any word from the original language. In this case, we need to understand exactly who was with God during the time he recreated the earth. Who are the "morning stars," and who are the "sons of God"? Jesus provided us with the answer concerning the "morning stars." "The mystery of the seven stars which thou sawest in my right hand, and the seven golden candlesticks. The seven stars are the angels of the seven churches;

and the seven candlesticks which thou sawest are the seven churches" (Revelation 1:20).

According to Jesus, stars represent angels. During this inquiry of Job, *morning* was added to the term *stars* to indicate time. The placement of souls in flesh bodies was the morning for man. We know that Jesus is the only begotten Son of God (John 1:18, John 3:16, 1 John 4:9). We also know that Jesus referred to himself as the Son of Man. "But that you may know that the Son of man hath power upon earth to forgive sins, (he said unto the sick of the palsy,) I say unto thee, Arise, and take up thy couch, and go into thine house" (Luke 5:24). Jesus applied the title "Son of Man" to himself instead of "Son of God." The title identifies not only the person but also the time. The title "Son of Man" refers to the time Jesus was on earth as the Savior in a flesh body. The title indicates both identity and time. The title "Son of Man" was the title showing Jesus was the fulfillment of the prophecy recorded in *Genesis 3:15*. Jesus referred back to the prophecy in Genesis in *John 5:46–47*.

When God told us that one-third of his angels followed Satan, they were also represented as stars *(Revelation 12:4)*. Notice that when God indicated the "sons of God," he said "all the sons of God." With the "morning stars," God did not indicate "all." Why? Some of the angels were not present. The rebellion of Satan had already taken place, and some of the angels chose to follow Satan instead of our Father. This fact is also how we determine that God, while talking to Job, was referring to recreation instead of the original creation. God made a point to indicate all his sons were present but not all the angels.

"For if God spared not the angels that sinned, but cast them down to hell, and delivered them into chains of darkness, to be reserved unto judgment" (2 Peter 2:4). The angels that rebelled were not present because they were bound in chains of darkness. God indicated all the sons were present, but not all the angels showing this was after the rebellion. Who were the "sons of God" present when God recreated the earth? "But as many as received him, to them gave the power to become the sons of God, even to them that believe on his name" (John 1:12). The beloved apostle John informed us that as many as received Jesus become the "sons of God." "For as many as are led by the Spirit of God, they are the sons of God" (Romans 8:14). Paul says if the Holy Spirit leads us, then we are the "sons of God."

A question you may have at this point might be, how can man be present with God before the earth was recreated? Jesus taught us that man has two bodies, a flesh body and a spiritual body housing the soul. Jesus said, "And fear not them which kill the body, but are not able to kill the soul: but rather fear him which is able to destroy both soul and body in hell" (Matthew 10:28).

Jesus warned not to fear people who may be able to kill the flesh body but rather fear God, who is able to kill the flesh body and the spiritual body housing our soul. Man in his spiritual body is not tied to earth. When our flesh body dies, our spiritual body returns to God, who gave it (Ecclesiastes 12:6–7 and 2 Corinthians 5:6–8). All souls belong to God, and all souls are the "sons of God." "Jesus answered them, is it not written in your law, I said, Ye are gods?" (John 10;34). Jesus is not saying (as some in the church say) that man is a god but is saying that man belongs to God, showing possession. Again, "I have said, Ye are Gods; and all of you are children of the most High" (Psalm 82:6). This is the verse Jesus referred to, and it clearly shows Jesus was showing possession and not that man is a god. "Behold, all souls are mine; as the soul of the father, so also the soul of the son is mine; the soul that sinneth, it shall die" (Ezekiel 18:4). Our Father, through Ezekiel, told us he owns all souls. Another question that might arise in your mind could be, why were the angels that rebelled not present during recreation but the souls of men that rebelled were present? Is this really fair of God? With wisdom and understanding, one can only conclude the answer to be yes. All men are the children of God. This includes the souls that rebelled following Satan as well as the ones that did not. When a child disobeys the parent, the child is still the parents' child. The child is punished for the purpose of correction but is still loved.

Angels were never children of God. They were and are servants. "But to which of the angels said he at any time, Sit on my right hand, until I make thine enemies thy footstool* Are they not all ministering spirits, sent forth to minister for them who shall be heirs of salvation?" (Hebrews 1:13–14). Paul was comparing angels to Jesus. Jesus was the only one our Father told to sit at his right hand. Jesus is the Son of God, so Paul was comparing angels to the sons of God. When we accept Jesus, we abide in him, making us his body. We are sitting on the right hand of God even as Jesus is!

Paul taught us that angels are ministering spirits, meaning servants. Paul also said they are our servants as well, taking orders from our Father on our behalf, until we return home. *(See Matthew 18:10.)*

When our Father commanded Jesus to be the redeeming sacrifice for man and prepared the earth for man to inhabit, he had a specific plan to follow. God knew the complete plan before creating flesh bodies for his children. This plan was not shared with the angels but is shared with all of God's children. The rebellious angels were cast from heaven along with Satan.

Our Father's plan provides the means to teach and correct our Father's rebellious children. The man that accepts our Father's grace through our savior, Jesus, the Christ, is the heir of salvation. All that man must do is hear the Word of God and accept the truth written therein, turn away from our rebellious ways, and return the love our Father has for us. It is our Father's will that all souls repent during their tour of duty in flesh bodies. This placement of souls into flesh bodies would be the very first time any child of God would be separated from our Father. A child spending the night at a friend's house for the first time may not stay all night. The child gets homesick and calls the parent to come after them. Parents are aware of this, and before the child is delivered to the friend, the parent will assure the child that everything is all right. The recreation process was a demonstration to all of God's sons that everything would be all right. This is why all of God's sons shouted for joy as they witnessed the recreation of the earth. All of God's sons that had rebelled would be given a chance to repent. They witnessed the love and care God took in the recreation of their new home. God revealed his power to recreate by the Word of his mouth to assure his children he has the power to protect them. He revealed his eternal love for them by the care taken in their provision. God misses his children in the same way the parent misses the child spending the night away from home for the first time. This explains why a thousand years with man is but one day with God. God's children are spending the night away from home for the first time. This does explain why a child of God talks about going home at the end of their lives here on earth. We all become aware of having lived with God before we came to live here on earth.

If the intention of our Father in Genesis was not to provide details of recreation, then what was God's intention? God wanted us to learn two things: First, God has the power to recreate using just the words of his mouth. God has no need to provide details because all of God's sons witnessed the power of his Word. Notice the repeated phrase "And God said." This phrase is repeated nine times in the first chapter of Genesis. Days 1–6 begin with this phrase. God clearly emphasized his power to recreate through the power of his Word, emphasizing his power to protect us even as we are separated. Notice also that when recreated by the power of his Word, God saw and it was good. This is to say, whatever his Word recreated was complete. God did not recreate and have to fix it, for it was good.

The most important lesson we can learn from all of God's Word is the revelation of his Son, Jesus Christ; Jesus is the Word of God. Consider this: every story, event, teaching, prophecy and every law, statute, and word of our Father recorded in the Old Testament points forward to the Son of Man.

Know this: every story, event, teaching, prophecy fulfilled, doctrine, and statues recorded in the New Testament points back to the Son of God. "I am Alpha and Omega, the beginning and the ending, saith the Lord, which is, and which was, and which is to come, the Almighty" (Revelation 1:8). *Jesus is the beginning, the end, and everything in between. Jesus is the Word, the life, the spring of living water, the bread of life, the consoler, the true vine, the great intercessor, the uplifted savior, and the victor over death.*

Every chapter in the gospel of John portrays Jesus in a different light. It is impossible to find one teaching in all of our Father's Word that is not in some way centered on Jesus. Every teaching either provides a different aspect of Jesus or explains why we need Jesus. *Jesus is Emmanuel (God with us).* "Then said I, Lo, I come (in the volume of the book it is written of me) to do thy will, O God" (Hebrews 10:7).

All the Word of God is written of Jesus! Understand this: every word given by our Father, every lesson learned from our Father, and every example provided by our Father is for the purpose of revealing his true nature to us through his Son, Jesus Christ. "But take ye heed; behold, I have foretold you all things" (Mark 13:23) There is nothing appropriate for the ears of man that Jesus has not foretold us. While reading any chapter of the Bible, if one is unable to find a tie to Jesus, in some way, reread it while asking our Father to show you his intention for giving that chapter. Never lose sight of our hero Jesus! Our savior came to do the will of our Father. The will of our Father was for Jesus to reveal the true nature of our Father to us and for Jesus to raise up all who believe in him on the last day *(John 6:38–40)*.

God is fighting a war on our behalf. The power to win this war he placed in his only begotten Son, Jesus Christ. The most important idea God wants man to understand is the consequences of this war and how he protects us from it. (This is Jesus.) This is, in fact, the very first thing God told us in the recreation account. Genesis 1:1 states God has the power to create, protect, and provide for man, and chapter 1, verse 2 shows what God is protecting us from. When God said he created the heavens and earth, he was saying our real home is in heaven with him but we must first travel through life on earth to learn the true nature of our Father as well as the nature of the one wishing to destroy us. Jesus actually taught us the same thing when he said, "And no man hath ascended up to heaven, but he that came down from heaven, even the Son of Man which is in heaven" (John 3:13). *Man did not just arrive on earth. We came from heaven.*

Jesus is telling us that by the time the Bible is complete, he is back in heaven and no one can get there without first traveling through this life. Many believe Jesus was only referring to himself in this verse. This is not the case because men return to God when their physical bodies die. At conception, God places the soul into the womb of the mother. This is how we come down from heaven. Our Father, through Solomon, told us again, "Or ever the silver cord be loosed, or the golden bowl be broken, or the pitcher be broken at the fountain, or the wheel broken at the cistern. Then shall the dust return to the earth as it was; and the spirit shall return unto God who gave it" (Ecclesiastes 12:6–7). *At the time of our death, our soul housed in the spiritual body returns to God who gave it.*

We could not return to God unless we came from God. God created both dwellings. Our Father is very careful to let us know that although we are separated from him at present, when our tour of duty is over, we are going home. Also, we are never truly separated from him. While we are on earth, we are never out of his sight. He watches over us, and at any time the need arises, he commands his servants (angels) to minister (serve) to us *(Matthew 18:10–14). The instant we choose our Father over Satan, the Holy Spirit enters us and we abide in Jesus.* We are never really away from our Father. You can talk to your Father right now. The truth is, you need not say a word with your lips. No one need hear your conversation. He is your Father. At any time if you will talk to him in your mind, he will hear. If you need faith to accept him and his Son, ask him for it. He is very intelligent and understanding and would love nothing more than to provide you with the faith to believe him. He loves you, but you must choose him.

Part One—Acts
"In the Beginning"
Eternity Past

> And the earth was without form, and void; and darkness was upon the face of the deep. And the Spirit of God moved upon the face of the waters. (Genesis 1:2)

This second verse is not a description of how God created the heaven and earth. This is a verse of symbolism. The key instructing us this is a verse of symbolism, which is the use of the word *face*. God was not speaking descriptively but was speaking symbolically. Ask yourself this question right now before reading further: knowing that God provided the exact details of the birth, life, death, and resurrection of our savior, Jesus Christ, even the exact words of Jesus on the cross, hundreds of years before it happened, if God was describing something as important as creation, do you believe his words would be vague? God did not say the earth had no form and it was empty and dark, thereby describing he said it had no form and was empty (void) and darkness was on the face of the deep and he moved on the face of the waters. These are the words of one speaking symbolically. By breaking this verse down and looking closely at its parts, we receive a wonderful revelation.

Part One—Acts
"In the Beginning"
Eternity Past

And the earth was without form, and void. (Genesis 1:2)

Earth #ra' erets ("eh-rets")—the Hebrew word translated *earth* in English is *erets*. The word comes from an old root word that means "to be firm." The earth or land, a wilderness world. *Erets* is also a Hebrew idiom meaning "common" and "nations." The Hebrew idiom means all other nations, the gentiles, or the common people as differentiated from the Hebrews. The Hebrew idiom provided through erets highlight the beginning of a very important truth taught throughout the word of God. There are but two types of people in the world, his kind (Jesus) and their kind (Satan), each having their own seed. All the races of the world, all people of the world, fit into one of these two categories. Are they his kind or their kind? Our Father does not recognize any race. They are all his children. When our Father created all the races on day 6, he looked and it was good. He loves us all. The only factor God sees is if they are his kind or their kind.

The definition for the word (*erets*) has not changed, although the word is no longer used; it means "to be firm." No object can be without form and firm at the same time. *Without form* means to offer no resistance to external pressure, while *firm* means to offer strong resistance to external pressure. This is not the earth in its natural state or the earth in the process of creation but is the earth in the midst of some catastrophic event. God did not create the earth with his hands having to shape the earth. God created the earth with his Word. Every time something was recreated by the power of God's Word, the object appeared perfect. Notice God repeatedly said, and God saw and it was good. Remember, he emphasized this so we would understand.

Part One—Acts
"In the Beginning"
Eternity Past

And the earth was without form, and void.
(Genesis 1:2)

Hayah ("haw-yaw")—the Hebrew word *Hayah* translated was in English means "to be, become, come to pass, exist" and, when used symbolically, means "altogether," "become" and "accomplished." The word is a root word and is always emphatic or, in other words, always expressed with emphasis. God chose this word in his sentence structure to place emphasis on the fact that the earth was not without form and void in the process of creation but that the earth became without form and void. Some event before the creation of man in flesh bodies caused the earth to become without form and void. God showed Jeremiah what this event was. As one reads the prophecies from God provided through Jeremiah, one quickly becomes awestruck by the very first words God spoke through him. They must have overwhelmed Jeremiah like a ton of bricks. God said, "Then the word of the Lord came unto me, saying, Before I formed thee in the belly I knew thee; and before thou camest forth out of the womb I sanctified thee, and I ordained thee a prophet unto the nations" (Jeremiah 1:4–5). These verses raise one big question: is God really saying he knew Jeremiah before he placed Jeremiah's soul into the womb of his mother? The answer is yes! We know that God created every soul, thereby knowing all souls. God not only knew the soul of Jeremiah but knew also the exact person Jeremiah would be as a man before Jeremiah was born. Before God placed Jeremiah into the womb, God knew him well enough to assign his duty as a prophet before his birth.

We have reached a point in this conversation (if you will allow me the freedom to use this term) where we need an answer to the question that arises as to how God knew Jeremiah before his birth. Let us think this through; since God puts the souls of each of us into the womb of the mother, there is only one way this could occur. The souls must be with God in order for him to accomplish this feat. We have no answer as to how long we were with God before we were born, but we clearly had to have been with him in order for him to have put our souls into the bodies that were in our mothers' wombs. We know the longer we are with someone, we begin to know that person, their personality, their thought pattern, what is important to them, and how they will react to any given circumstance. Considering God is so much better at this than we are, it is no wonder God knows just how each of us will react to every event in our lives.

If God assigned Jeremiah his duties, then it makes it clear that he assigns each of us our duties as well. If God assigns us our duties, he knows us well enough to know that we are quite capable of fulfilling our assignments.

"I beheld the earth, and lo, it was without form, and void; and the heavens, and they had no light" (Jeremiah 4:23). Jeremiah brings the reader back to Genesis. Jeremiah brings us back to the account of recreation by using the same phrase "was without form and void." Jeremiah beheld and said the heavens had not light. Jeremiah is saying the sun, the moon, and stars were gone, leaving earth in total darkness for an extended period of time. In God's Word, there are times when God darkened the day, but not with the removal of the sun, moon, and stars for an extended period of time. Read the first five verses in Genesis making up the first day of recreation and you will see that this is the time when the heavens had no light, and it is the only time. The heavens having no light instructs us Jeremiah was referring to time before man arrived on earth in flesh bodies. God is light, and man in spiritual bodies with God needs no light. Lights were created on day 4, while flesh bodies for man were made on day 6. At the end of this earth age, Jesus returns and Jesus is the

Light. Since man was placed on earth, never was there a time when all of man was in complete darkness or never shall there be. Man in the flesh has never witnessed the sky without the sun or moon. God is about to tell us through Jeremiah the event that happened was, in fact, God destroying the first earth age.

> I beheld the mountains, and lo, they trembled, and all the hills moved lightly I beheld, and lo, there was no man, and all the birds of the heavens were fled I beheld, and lo, the fruitful place was a wilderness, and all the cities thereof were broken down at the presence of the LORD, and by his fierce anger. (Jeremiah 4:24–26)

God, in his fierce anger, shook the earth and, in fact, destroyed the first earth age. The apostle Paul teaches us in the twelfth chapter of Hebrews to hold on to Jesus through chastisement, because that is proof that God loves us. You only correct the ones you love. By the end of the chapter, Paul teaches us that God shook and destroyed the first earth age.

> See that ye refuse not him that speaketh. For if they escaped not who refused him that spake on earth, much more shall not we escape, if we turn away from him that speaketh from heaven: Whose voice then shook the earth; but now he hath promised, saying, Yet once more I shake not the earth only, but also heaven. And this word, Yet once more, signifieth the removing of those things that are shaken, as of things that are made, that those things which cannot be shaken may remain. (Hebrews 12:25–27)

If we now refuse him (Jesus), he will shake the earth again along with heaven and we shall not escape the destruction of this earth age.

The church would say Paul was referring to the time God spoke when Jesus gave up the Ghost on the cross. The problem with this is, at this time our Father may have been sad, but not in fierce anger. Remember, this is the time our Father tore the veil of the temple, giving access to him for all. The shaking of the earth did not result in the cities of the earth being broken down. Also, Paul said the ones that refused Jesus did not escape the shaking of the earth, making it past tense. Jeremiah plainly states God shook the earth in his fierce anger, destroying the first earth, breaking down all cities of earth.

In order for a pilot to fly an airplane, a pilot's license is required. The license is not issued without first the pilot demonstrating his ability safely take off, fly, and land the aircraft. Testing is also required to demonstrate the pilot's ability to correctly navigate. Many hours of safely flying and navigating must be recorded before testing. Pilots are taught that true north and magnetic north are ninety miles apart.

Why? Because God shook this earth in his anger, resulting in the tilting of the earth. The statement "And the earth was without form, and void" was the way our Father decided to inform us in Genesis that he had destroyed the earth, resulting in the destruction of the first earth age. What could have been the cause for such anger expressed by our Father? The next portion of the same verse in Genesis provides the answer.

Part One—Acts
"In the Beginning"
Eternity Past

And darkness was upon the face of the deep.
(Genesis 1:2)

This portion of this verse is the key explaining the entire verse. *Darkness* was upon the *face* of the deep. It is obvious the deep is referring to water—"The Spirit of God moved upon the face of the waters" (Genesis 1:2). When one stands over a clear pool of water, whose face is seen in the water?

The face reflected will always be the face of the one observing. The face of the water changes as the humans observing it change. The face in the water has a strong lure, and man can at times be hypnotizing with the power to hold the observer. The face of the waters is the face of man. The human body is made up of about 80 percent water. Man cannot live without water. God symbolically tells us that darkness was upon all the sons of God, threatening them. Water symbolically represents man. We find this to be true in the book of Revelation.

This is one book of the Bible written more in symbolism than in prose. "And he saith unto me, The waters which thou sawest, where the whore sitteth are peoples, and multitudes, and nations, and tongues" (Revelation 17:15). This representation of man referred to as water was also seen in Revelation 20:13—"And the sea gave up the dead which were in it; and death and hell delivered up the dead which were in them; and they were judged every man according to their works." God would never put a soul in hell before that soul was judged. God does not take people out of hell to judge them and return them to hell. This is a verse of symbolism. The sea giving up the dead means the sea is all nations, and giving up the dead is the spiritually dead. Death and hell is the location the spiritually dead go, not the location of them at this time. *(Read Luke 16 and Revelation 20.)* If man is sentenced to hell, the result is death of the soul *(Matthew 10:28)*. God also uses clouds to represent man. What are clouds? Water! Clouds are a visible body of very fine water droplets or ice particles suspended in the atmosphere at altitudes ranging up to several miles above sea level. This representation of man by the use of clouds can be found in the book of Hebrews.

"Wherefore seeing we also are compassed about* with so great a cloud of witnesses, let us lay aside every weight, and the sin which doth so easily beset us, and let us run with patience the race that is set before us" (Hebrews 12:1). Had Paul, in the use of cloud, been referring to nature witnessing to man, surely he would have not limited nature to a single cloud. A single cloud may be used to teach a single aspect of God's provision for man but not the full gospel of Jesus. The teaching of the gospel of Jesus would require all of nature.

Again, in the book of Revelation, John symbolically refers to man as clouds. "Behold, he cometh with clouds; and every eye shall see him, and they also which pierced him: and all kindreds of the earth shall wail because of him. Even so, A-men" (Revelation 1:7). When John said Jesus is coming with clouds, notice it was plural cloud and not singular, as was used by Paul. The number of people returning with Jesus is so great they could not be contained in a single cloud. When God said that darkness was upon the face of the deep, God was clearly stating that darkness was upon the sons of God. When God chose John to pen the book of Revelation, like Jeremiah God knew John, God knew John before he was placed in the womb of his mother. The beloved Apostle John was also chosen to pen the three epistles of John. The apostle John demonstrated his understanding of the first chapter of Genesis and directly explained this time before the first day in Genesis. John, through the book of Revelation, gave us the meaning of the waters in the second verse in Genesis. The gospel of John identifies for us the meaning of darkness. The very first words in the gospel of John send us back to the beginning.

> In the beginning was the Word, and the Word was with God, and the Word was God. The same was in the beginning with God. All things were made by him; and without him was not anything made that was made. In him was life; and the life was the light of men. And the light shineth in darkness; and the darkness comprehended it not. (John 1:1–5)

Notice all this happened in the beginning. As has already been stated, the most important lesson to be learned in all of God's Word is the revelation of Jesus Christ. John understood this and penned the only gospel that highlights a different aspect of Jesus in each chapter. The very first words in the gospel of John reveal Jesus Christ as *the Word*. The very next thing God tells us is that Jesus Christ made all things. God continues by telling us that Jesus Christ is *life* and that *life* is the *light of men*. Notice the very next thing revealed is that *light* shown in darkness and darkness comprehended it not.

Compare these verses with the first five verses in Genesis. First the *Word of God* is our Father's declaration of creation in Genesis 1:1. This declaration is that God loves his children, protects, and provides for them and Jesus is *the Word*. The entire Bible was written explaining this declaration seen in Genesis 1:1. Next, notice, literally, the first words our Father spoke in Genesis 1:3, compared to John's teaching in Jesus, was *life* and that *life* was the *light of men*. John continues and says that *light* was shown in darkness and darkness comprehended it not. Unless these words are spoken symbolically, they cannot be true. True darkness always yields to light. Walk in any dark room and turn on the light. Darkness is gone. Light destroyed the darkness. Darkness cannot comprehend anything. It has no mind to understand or comprehend with. Comprehension can only be realized by a living entity with a mind. Who is the antithesis of God and Jesus? The answer, of course, is Satan. The living entity that refuses to repent or comprehend "the light" is Satan. God, through the beloved apostle John, has identified for us the darkness of Genesis 1:2.

"For God so loved the world, that he gave his only begotten Son, that whosoever believeth in him should not perish, but have everlasting life" (John 3:16). This verse is memorized by more people than any other verse in the Word of God. Jesus told us that our Father loves us so much that he was willing to allow his only begotten Son to be the sacrifice one time for whosoever will to be saved. The very next words of Jesus teach us that he did not come into the world to condemn the world. "For God sent not his Son into the world to condemn the world; but that the world through him might be saved" (John 3:17). Jesus came to save us! The next thing that Jesus said was, he is the only way! "He that believeth on him is not condemned: but he that believeth not is condemned already, because he hath not believed in the name of the only begotten Son of God" (John 3:18). Jesus is not telling us what this condemnation is in this verse. He is telling us that we are condemned already and, if we refuse him, we are still condemned. The very next verse informs us why we are condemned.

"And this is the condemnation, that light is come into the world, and men loved darkness rather than light, because their deeds were evil" (John 3:19). "For everyone that doeth evil hateth the light, neither* cometh to the light, lest his deeds should be reproved" (John 3:20). What is darkness? Evil! What is evil, or who is evil? Satan. What did Jesus call himself? Light. Jesus clearly states that man has the choice. In Jesus's first lesson, he taught us that he is the light and evil or Satan is darkness. Understanding this must be of utmost importance for it to be the first lesson Jesus taught as well as the first thing our Father taught in Genesis. With the understanding of the teaching of the beloved apostle John that Jesus is the Word and understanding the first teaching of Jesus that he is the light and Satan is the darkness, we can better understand the second verse of Genesis chapter one. Genesis 1:1 declares God loves us and has power to protect us. Verse 2 explains what God is protecting us from. God is protecting us from darkness, which is Satan. By examining the rest of verse 2, we can see how God protected us.

Part One—Acts
"In the Beginning"
Eternity Past

And the Spirit of God moved upon the face
of the waters. (Genesis 1:2)

Moved @xr *Rachaph* ("raw-kha!")—the Hebrew word translated *moved* in English is *Rachaph*. This is a prime root and means "to brood." When this word is used, it also implies "to shake, flutter, and move." "To brood" means "to protect (young) by or as if covering with the wings," "to hover enveloping, loom," and "to focus the attention on a subject persistently and moodily," "worry." We have already seen that the face of the waters represents all of God's children. The use of the Hebrew word *Rachaph* truly provides the appropriate description of our Father's worry for his children as well as his love and protection. He was facing something completely new to all. Never before had war been declared, and never before was there a threat to God's children. The path made by God was, in fact, made without any errors and was made with wisdom *(Proverbs 8:22–30)*. The answer demanded our hero, Jesus Christ. The very next verse in the account of recreation in Genesis tells us that indeed our hero Jesus Christ was, in fact, that perfect answer.

Part One—Acts
"In the Beginning"
Day One

> And God said, Let there be light; and there was light. (Genesis 1:3)

Genesis 1:3 actually is the start of day 1. Notice chapters 1–6 started with the phrase "And God said." Like Genesis 1:1, this third verse is a declaration by God. The first declaration declared God created heaven and earth through the power of his Word.

This second declaration declared that Jesus is, in fact, needed to win this war. And God said, "Let there be Jesus." Like verse 1, this verse also provides the information required filling volumes of literary books. Understanding the first day presented in Genesis answers one of the first questions that I have had most of my life—that is, since light was on day 4 and this is day 1, what is this light? God had no need to run and get a flashlight. God is a consuming fire, and fire produces light (Hebrews 12:29). God, through Paul, explained to us exactly what the light of verse 3 was when Paul was writing to the church in Corinth. "For God, who commanded the light to shine out of darkness*, hath shined in our hearts, to give the light of the knowledge of the glory of God in the face of Jesus Christ" (2 Corinthians 4:6). Notice Paul first sends us back to the beginning. Paul also used the same terminology, use of face, darkness, and light. Paul was actually referring to this third verse in Genesis when saying God commanded the light to shine out of darkness. Paul was saying that Jesus is the light but it takes more; one must have the knowledge of the glory of God, and this is that God is a forgiving god through our hero, Jesus Christ. This is to say that knowing that Jesus is the

Son of God is not enough. All of Satan's demons as well as Satan know Jesus is the Son of God.

One must recognize the need for salvation, repent for their rebellious ways, and accept Jesus for their salvation. Man must choose God! This can only be done when God calls you. This is when God shines in our hearts, giving the light of the knowledge of the glory of God. Again, that Glory of God is that he forgives through his Son, Jesus Christ. This is the true nature of God. The Holy Spirit enters you and convicts your heart, telling you that these words are true, and asks you to accept salvation. The Holy Spirit speaks to you from within. This is the true light, the light that will never leave you in darkness. When one receives this light, you can feel the warmth of our Father's hugs as he welcomes us back. This is not to say that life is over at this point; just the opposite is true. Life has just begun, and there is much work to be done. Our Father will lead you hand in hand gently in wisdom, love, and mercy, providing the help needed to accomplish the goals he has set for you. As we abide in him, we realize this is true peace and nothing can separate us from our Father's love and protection.

Part One—Acts
"In the Beginning"
Day One

And God saw the light, that it was good;
and God divided* the light from the darkness.
(Genesis 1:4)

With the understanding of the identity of the light and the darkness, it is easy to understand the dividing of the light from the darkness. God separated the souls that followed Satan from the souls that stayed with him, making a stand against Satan. God created a gulf that cannot be passed and placed the souls following Satan on one side of the gulf. The throne of God and all the souls staying with our Father is on the other side of the gulf. This was done for the protection of the souls that made a stand with our Father against Satan.

The only way to be on the right side of this gulf is to accept Jesus as your personal savior in this lifetime when God calls you. If God is calling you now, accept him as your personal God and savior. You do not know how many times God will call you to repentance. Confess your sins now and get started on your way to heaven.

Jesus taught us of this gulf, and we can read the account of his teachings in the gospel of *Luke 16:19.*

> There was a certain rich man, which was clothed in purple and fine linen, and fared sumptuously every day, And there was a certain beggar named Lazarus, which was laid at his gate, full of sores, and desiring to be fed with the crumbs which fell from the rich man's table; moreover the dogs came and licked his sores. And it came to pass, that the beggar died, and was carried by the angels into Abraham's bosom; the rich man also died, and was buried; And in hell he lift up his eyes, being in torments, and seeth Abraham afar off, and Lazarus in his bosom. And he cried and said, Father Abraham, have mercy on me, and send Lazarus, that he may dip the tip of his finger in water, and cool my tongue; for I am tormented in this flame. But Abraham said, Son, remember that thou in thy lifetime received thy good things, and likewise Lazarus evil things; but now he is comforted, and thou art tormented. And beside all this, between us and you there is a great gulf fixed; so they which would pass from hence to you cannot*; neither can they pass to us, that would come from thence. Then he said, I pray thee therefore, father, that thou wouldest send him to my father's house; For I have five brethren; that he may testify unto them, lest they also come into this place of torment. Abraham saith unto him, They have Moses and the proph-

ets; let them hear them, And he said, but if one went unto them from the dead, they will repent. And he said unto him, if they hear not Moses and the prophets, neither will they be persuaded, though one rose from the dead. (Luke 16:19–31)

There is so much taught in these verses on so many different levels it would take books to teach them all. For our purpose, first notice the rich man was not really in hell. Hell is the place that destroys both body and soul *(Matthew 10:28)*. The torment of the rich man was waking up dead realizing he had not accepted salvation. This is real torment from within. Notice also the beggar's name was Lazarus. Lazarus represents all that are saved. The name Lazarus means "who God helps." God does not want anyone to end up on the wrong side of this gulf. It is the will of God that all men come to repentance and receive salvation *(2 Peter 3:9)*. Notice that nothing prevented the souls on the wrong side of the gulf from seeing Abraham. This tells us that they can still see our Father and his throne. Communication across the gulf is also possible. Jesus, at the time of this teaching, had yet to be crucified. After his crucifixion, Jesus did rise from the dead after three days and did testify to man of these truths. During the three days Jesus's body was supposedly in the tomb, he went to the gulf preaching and many were saved *(1 Peter 3:18–20)*. There are many within the church that teach this gulf does not exist. They say because Jesus spoke in parables this is not to be taken literally. I choose to believe the words of Jesus instead of the traditions of man. God has never approved of the traditions of man. In fact, Jesus always condemned the traditions of man. The disciples of Jesus asked him why he spoke in parables. "And the disciples came, and said unto him, Why speaketh thou unto them in parables? He answered and said unto them, Because it is given unto you to know the mysteries of the kingdom of heaven, but to them it is not given" (Matthew 13:10–11). Notice Jesus did not say the reason was to prevent his words from being interpreted literally. Jesus often spoke in parables and explained the reason. Those in darkness, through the use of parables, are kept in darkness. This verse also verifies our understanding that the servants (angels) that rebelled were not with God during recreation. To them is not given to know the mysteries of the kingdom of heaven. To the seed of Satan, it is not given either. Without eyes to see and ears to hear, darkness is all that can be comprehended.

They are those who teach the traditions of man. They will remain in darkness unless our Father gives them eyes to see and ears to hear. Those with ears to hear and eyes to see understand the mysteries of God through the use of parables.

> Part One—Acts
> "In the Beginning"
> Day One

> And God called the light Day, and the darkness he called Night, And the evening and the morning were the first day. (Genesis 1:5)

We are the children of the day. The children of Satan are the children of the night. This is the completion of day 1 and, in fact, was a very busy day.

This is not the first day for our planet. Heaven and earth were not created on the first day but were rejuvenated after the destruction of the first earth age. God did not tell us when he created the heaven and the earth. Most scientists agree that the earth is millions of years old. When the Word of God is understood, it provides nothing to dispute their claim and, in fact, supports the theory. Eternity past includes Satan's rebellion with God destroying the first earth age. God shook this earth when the destroyer threatened all of God's sons. God brooded over his children while deciding on the solution to this problem. Through wisdom, God decided to regenerate the earth and commanded our hero, Jesus, to pay the price for treason. This started day 1. God is about to create flesh bodies for his sons and send them to live on earth learning the true nature of him as well as the nature of the evil one. This is a choice everyone must make: Satan and death, or eternal life with our loving Father. The choice is yours to make. Putting it off and never making the choice is, in fact, the choice to stay condemned with Satan. This choice can be made right now. One need not be at a church or have anyone with you. The choice is made in your heart. One needs only to choose God in your heart and ask him for the faith to accept him and our hero, Jesus Christ. Jesus already paid the price on the cross for you. Accept it in your heart, for that is all that is required. The rest is up to God. With long-suffering, he will gently lead you into his Word and give you the understanding that you may need. If you love him and want to be with him, he will never leave you or let you down in any way. He loves you very much and wants so much for you to love him in return. Never has a man wooed a woman the way God is wooing all his children.

Part One—Acts
"In the Beginning"
Day Two

> And God said, Let there be a firmament in the midst of the waters, and let it divide the waters from the waters. And God made the firmament, and divided the waters which were under the firmament from the waters which were above the firmament: and it was so. And God called the firmament Heaven. And the evening and the morning were the second day. (Genesis 1:6–8)

Question: if this is the description of the creation process, what did the description of day 2 answer for us concerning creation? The second day of recreation was another demonstration by our Father of his love and protection assuring all his children that everything would be all right. This demonstration is seen in the recreation of the earth's atmosphere. This is the seat providing life-sustaining water as well as oxygen for man to breathe. This is a perpetual provision for man by God. The cycle of water evaporating and returning to earth gently provides water for all. The relationship of men with plants accepting man's exhaled carbon dioxide and returning pure oxygen each provide life for the other. The air that man breathes also represents the Holy Spirit. Just as the air is shared with all men, the Holy Spirit is here for every man. The Holy Spirit was given for man before man was created, eliminating the possibility for any man not to have access to him. This is another demonstration for all of God's children that God is with us. Don't try to run and hide from God; rather run to God. The atmosphere provides gentle breezes to cool man as well as protection from harmful ultraviolet rays. A foreign object attempting to enter this protective layer from space is, upon entry, incinerated. Witness the shooting star, God took great care to reveal his eternal love for man. Day 2, through our Father's choice of words, reaffirms that this is a day of recreation and not creation.

Part One—Acts
"In the Beginning"
Day Two

Created *arb Bara'* ("haw-raw'")—the Hebrew word *Bara* translated created in the first verse of the Bible tells an illuminating story within itself. The definition is to shape, fashion, and create. The light is yielded with the understanding of its use. It is used only with God as the subject. The Hebrew language demands it. God is the only one with the power to truly create. *Bara* means to create out of nothing. The ability man has to create is limited to the shaping or forming a material. Man has no power to create out of nothing. This is reserved for God.

When God told us, on day 2, that he made the atmosphere, the Hebrew word God chose was *hX['asah (aw-saw')*, having the opposite effect on the reader. *Asah* means to do, fashion, accomplish, and make. The use of this word is not restricted to our Father as the subject; the opposite is true. *Asah* is used in the widest sense with creation never implied. If day 2 was, in fact, addressing the original creation, *Bara* would have been used for the creation of our atmosphere. Since there is no oxygen for man to breathe outside the earth's atmosphere, we know God had to create it and place it here. The shooting star also provides a visual spiritual teaching. Stars are God's representation of his servants, the angels. The fallen angels were incarcerated to be reserved unto judgment. After judgment, they are incinerated in the lake of fire *(2 Peter 2:4 and Revelation 20:1–15)*. The shooting star is a pictorial of the fallen angels incinerated in the lake of fire. When we witness a shooting star, it is the end of time for that star. We are seeing it being incinerated. The pictorial of fallen stars (angels) is of their end. We should heed the warning. God uses the same term, *the fallen stars*, describing the angels (his servants) that rebelled with Satan.

One additional truth that can be highlighted on day 2 is the fact that the earth was also flooded. This reassures us that our understanding of God destroying the first earth age by shaking the earth was, as taught by Peter, also flooded *(2 Peter 3:5–6)*.

Part One—Acts
"In the Beginning"
Day Three

> And God said, Let the waters under the heaven be gathered together unto one place, and let the dry land appear; and it was so. And God called the dry land Earth; and the gathering together of the waters called he Seas; and God saw that it was good. And God said, Let the earth bring forth grass, the herb yielding seed, and the fruit tree yielding fruit after his kind, whose seed is in itself, upon the earth; and it was so. And the earth brought forth grass, and herb yielding seed after his kind, and the tree yielding fruit, whose seed was in itself, after his kind; and God saw that it was good. And the evening and the morning were the third day. (Genesis 1:9–13)

If the account of day 3 is a description of the process by which the heaven and earth were created, the account creates more questions than it answers. When the waters gathered together, why did they gather to one location? Was this location the lowest surface on earth? Why? Could God not have placed this location in a different spot? I love surfer music, so why did you not place the seas adjacent to my hometown so I could have learned to surf? Why does green grass turn brown when it's dying?

Why is the living grass green? I like purple! Why did you create grass that had to be cut and cared for? I work so many hours I must pay a neighborhood youth to tend my lawn. Didn't you think of this? You sure weren't thinking of me, were you? Why is the sky painted blue yet turns disgustingly gray during storms? I really don't like gray, and what's up with this red sky?

God had an excellent reason for not describing the creation process. The condition of man left God no choice but to leave out the account. A description of creation would have opened the door for critical questions and remarks from every generation, Man has no right to ask God how or why the choices were made concerning any aspect of creation. Can man duplicate any act of creation? Does man have power to create (*Bara*) out of nothing? Should God change color perception for each human? God took great care in the aesthetics of man's home, and still man throws trite questions and remarks at him. There would be no end to man's demonstration of his stiff-necked, egotistical ways had God described creation. God knew exactly what man needed to know, and that is what our Father told us. Remember, Jesus said that he has foretold us all things *(Mark 13:23)*. Jesus highlighted the beauty in the field while teaching his disciples not to worry. "Consider the lilies how they grow; they toil not, they spin not; and yet I say unto you, that Solomon in all his glory was not arrayed like one of these" (Luke 12:27).

Part One—Acts
"In the Beginning"
Day Four

> And God said, Let there be lights in the firmament of the heavens to divide the day from

the night; and let them be for signs, and for seasons, and for days and years; And let them be for lights in the firmament of the heaven to give light upon the earth; and it was so. And God made two great lights; the greater light to rule the day, and the lesser light to rule the night; he made the stars also. And God set them in the firmament of the heaven to give light upon the earth, And to rule over the night, and divide the light from the darkness; and God saw that it was good. And the evening and the morning were the fourth day. (Genesis 1:14–19)

Day 4 reaffirms our understanding of day 1. The dividing of the light from darkness on day 1 is not the same as provided on day 4. Day 4 brought the sun, moon, and stars to provide light on earth. Day 1 brought the light of the knowledge of the glory of God in the face of Jesus Christ providing light to the soul. Try to imagine a world of complete darkness. Shut your eyes and experience the world of the blind. The slightest accomplishment must be achieved without sight. The smile of a child could not be seen. Tears shed in joy fall but not seen. The only color perceived is the combination of all colors, black. The beauties of the mountains, ocean shores, sky, setting sun, falling leaves, and colors of the rainbow could not be appreciated through sight. The beauty of nature heard but not seen. Our Father had a wonderful purpose for the creation of lights in the heavens. God wanted man to experience the beauty of his creations. This is our Father's way of demonstrating to his children the power, graciousness, love, and beauty that is our Father. One can be captivated by the colors of the changing leaves as color shades make each setting uniquely different, each adding its special touch to the canvas. The beauty of our home changes with the season, and each is more beautiful than the previous one. Our home has withstood over six thousand years of man's pollution and rebellion, and still to its beauty nothing can compare. Now shut your spiritual eyes and experience the world of the spiritual blind. No beauty heard or seen. No tenderness, no hugs, no mercies, no peace, no rest, no laughter, no understanding, no love, no life is theirs. Rich with pride, with arrogance, with offense, with distrust, with slander, with lies, with thefts, with murders, with hate, and with death. Life for the spiritually blind is nothing more than a mere existence waiting on the executioner list. It is often too easy to find oneself angry toward the spiritually blind when truth teaches us to forgive. With insight to their life, forgiveness comes easier. Our Father wishes for all to open their spiritual eyes and see a world of love. Jesus paid the price of forgiveness for all. Open your spiritual eyes enough to take a look. Find what you have been missing; with it comes joy.

When our Father placed lights in the heavens, his purpose was manifold. In addition to providing light, the sun, moon, and stars give man the sense of time. Tilling the earth, planting, and harvesting each own their season. The measurement of time allows man to prepare for events bringing organization to life. No goal set is achieved without proper time management. The sun, moon, and stars were given also to rule day and night and for signs. God's Word tells us the sun rules the day and the moon rules the night. This is the perfect example for man to learn of Jesus and Satan. The spiritual truth taught on day 4 is a fortified reminder of day 1. The sun brings warmth and health to man, providing light that touches the soul. Nothing is hidden, exposing lessons of life. Man is capable of seeing death in its season as well as new life at its birth. Man can feel the gentle rays of the sun caressing the back of the neck, knowing its touch is the love of Jesus. The sun provides nutrients and is required for life. Jesus heals the sick and is required for everlasting life. The light of the sun shows man his way. The light of Jesus is the only way. The power of the sun is fire.

The power of Jesus is a righteous, sinless, just, and holy life. The sun is about ninety-three million miles away, yet we feel its touch. Jesus is in heaven, and we live because of his touch. The mass of the sun is three hundred thirty-three thousand times that of the earth, yet its light is shared with only one half of the earth at a time. Jesus is in heaven, yet everyone on earth can share his love and attention at the same time. The moon is the complete opposite of the sun. The sun is light. The moon has no light.

The light of the moon is only a reflection of the sun shining on the earth. The moon must take light from the sun, while Satan tries to steal light from the Son. The sun has perpetual life, while the moon (Satan) has no life. The sun has the power to provide all on earth life, while the moon (Satan) steals life. The only power the moon has is to pull on the earth. During the full moon, the tide on the seashore will rise as much as five feet. Satan pulls and tries to take all that belongs to our Father. The sun, moon, and stars were also provided for signs. We have already seen that the stars are a representation of the angels. Jesus used the sun, moon, and stars for a sign of his glorious Second Coming *(Matthew 24:29–30)*. Luke used the sun and the moon as a sign of the approaching day of the Lord *(Acts 2:20)*. The prophet Joel provides us with these signs also *(Joel chapters 2 and 3)*. The book of Revelation uses the sun, moon, and stars as signs to declare events quickly approaching. Our Father, on day 4, truly had all his children in mind and gave great gifts presented with love.

Part One—Acts
"In the Beginning"
Day Five

And God said, Let the waters bring forth abundantly the moving creature that hath life, and fowl that may fly above the earth in the open firmament of heaven. And God created great whales, and every living creature that moveth which the waters brought forth abundantly, after their kind, and every winged fowl after his kind; and God saw that it was good. And God blessed them, saying, Be fruitful, and multiply, and fill the waters in the seas, and let fowl multiply in the earth. And the evening and the morning were the fifth day. (Genesis 1:20–23)

Day 5 brought forth the treasures of the seas as well as colors of flight. Tropical fish seem to be florescent in the water as fowl dot the sky with color. The pride of the peacock as well as the blue jay and redbird are witnesses to our Father's love for beauty in color. Homes painted with warm, friendly colors truly help welcome a stranger. Fish of the seas and fowl created on the same day naturally go together. They fit like a hand in glove. The artist rendition using oil on canvas of the coast without seagulls produces a sense of famine. The coastline is a smorgasbord of delicacies provided by our Father for his fowl of the air. Fowl and fish fit together like a hand in glove. *Not!* The only time they really fit like a hand in glove is when fowl eats fish. Neither can live in the other's environment. So why did I contradict myself? The statement that they fit together seemed to be true. They were, after all, created on the same day. Be very careful with what seems to be the truth. Fish were created after their kind. Fowl was created after his kind.

Man is being delivered to man's friend and is spending the night at the friend's home. Man is in the kingdom of the friend. The problem is, man's friend is Satan. He would be quite happy if man would live with him forever. Problem is, he lies to man to keep man with him saying our Father abandoned him. The Word of God is used by Satan taking a truth and adding the slightest lie to it, making the complete statement a lie. This is how Satan works on all of us. Be very careful about what appears to be the truth. It is often a lie.

The surface of our earth is over 70 percent oceans, including the frozen North and South Poles. The sea provides a great wealth of life-sustaining food as well as valuable gems such as the black pearl increased in value because of its rarity. The sea is rich but was created after their king. The kingdom of Satan has many riches to invite one to stay but was created after their kind. The intelligence of dolphins allows their use by militaries of the world to save lives during war. In addition to carrying messages, dolphins are used by our military to locate mines placed in the sea by our enemies. The authority of the great white shark to swim in locations of its choice would seldom be challenged by the casual swimmers. Great sea monsters live in folklore creating bursts of excitement in our youth, while seniors exchange fish tales, each greater than the last. The treasures of the seas are truly immense. Our Father used a large fish for transporting the prophet Jonah, riding in the stomach of a great fish three days and nights, being delivered to Nineveh *(Jonah chapters 1–3)*. Fish were created after their kind. When Jesus called the brothers Peter and Andrew to be his disciples, they were fishing. Jesus told them to follow him and he would make them fishers of men *(Matthew 4:4–20)*. Fish were created after their kind. Spiritual teachings provided by living creatures of the seas are often seen in God's Word and would require a book to teach all levels taught by them. Fowl of the air are also used to teach spiritual truths. Fowl were created after his kind. God used the dove representing the Holy Spirit while teaching us the Trinity *(Matthew 3:16–17)*.

Day 1 presented God brooding over his children. The association tied to brooding is of the hen protecting her chicks *(Matthew 23:37–39)*. Our Father compared himself to an eagle describing his delivering Israel out of Egypt *(Exodus 19:4)*. Fowl were created after his kind. Throughout the Word of God, we find nature repeatedly used to teach man spiritual truths. God's use of nature to teach a spiritual truth can be seen by examining days 3, 5, and 6 together paying close attention to the repeated phrases "his kind" and "their kind." Repeated phrases should always alert the reader to a truth emphasized and taught. The statement has already been stated that the most important lesson learned in all of God's Word is the revelation of our hero Jesus Christ. While reading a chapter in the Word of God, if you are unable to find a tie to Jesus, in some way, reread it while asking our Father what his intention was for delivering that chapter. Nothing spoken by God compares to the significance of the glory in the face of Jesus Christ. His Word is Jesus Christ; God, throughout his Word, teaches this in many different ways.

Some verses are the words of our Father spoken succinctly (clear, precise expression in few words), directly providing the lesson. Other verses instruct by symbolism or poetry. A single verse may have many different truths taught, each with varying degrees of significance. God uses numbers to teach man also. Each number has its own meaning. The study of the way God uses numbers and their meaning can be called biblical mathematics.

While searching God's Word for the understanding of part 1 of the revelation I received, the Holy Spirit showed me the phrase "his kind" was a direct reference to Jesus. The phrase "their kind" was a direct reference to Satan. After I began to understand biblical mathematics, I understood the direct references even better. On day 3, we find the phrase "his kind" repeated three times referring to three things. The number 3 means divine completeness and perfection. This may be seen in the Trinity. The direct objects this phrase referred to on day 3 were grass, herbs, and fruit trees. By the phrase "his kind" being repeated three times on day 3 referring to three things, we see the objects being created were complete. The number 3 also means resurrection. On day 3, there is no reference made to their kind, no resurrection for their kind, just judgment, then death. Before the war of rebellion, there was only "his kind," and "their kind" did not exist.

The word *seed* was repeated four times, and 4 is the number meaning "creation" and "world." The seed of God (his kind), Jesus and man, would have to come into the world. The seed being in itself teaches the alert reader that the evolution theories are in fact just theories and not truth. Remember the word *seed*; it will gain in significance. Day 5 also presents the phrases "his kind" and "their kind." Each phrase is used once. This is the first time their kind was present. The war is now started.

The number 5 means grace. Grace is God's answer to the war and is provided to all his kind through him (Jesus), and we are only his kind by coming to God by Jesus Christ. Grace was presented on day 5, one day before man was created in flesh bodies. Man was created on day 6. Jesus was ordained before the foundation of the earth. Grace is reserved for "his kind." Remember on day 5 both phrases appeared once. The number 1 means unity. All their kind stands in unity against all that receive grace.

"But when the fullness of the time was come, God sent forth his Son, made of a woman, made under the law, To redeem them that were under the law, that we might receive the adoption of sons"

(Galatians 4:4–5). Jesus came made of a woman, meaning the seed of the woman—not the man and woman, but the seed of the woman only. Jesus came through a virgin birth. Jesus is the result of God and the woman. Mary received the baby Jesus as the result of the Holy Spirit coming upon her and placing the baby into her womb. This is why Jesus referred to himself as the Son of Man. Notice our Father's words delivered to Satan after the fall of man. God was, in fact, letting the devil know that he had a plan to deliver his people from the plans and actions of Satan while letting Satan know who would deliver that blow: God's only begotten Son, Jesus Christ. Jesus was and always has been the glory of his Father, willing to do whatever it takes to deliver the sons of God into their safe place. I have heard it said that Satan was not aware how Jesus would save his children. It would not have made any difference if he had known. Greater is he that is in me than he that is in the world. Amen. Notice our Father's words delivered to Satan after the fall of man. "And I will put enmity between thee and the woman, and between thy seed and her seed; it shall bruise thy head; and thou shalt bruise his heel" (Genesis 3:15).

Part One—Acts
"In the Beginning"
Day Six

> And God said, Let the earth bring forth the living creature after his kind, cattle, and creeping things, and beast of the earth after his kind; and it was so. And God made the beast of the earth after his kind; and it was so. And God made the beast of the earth after his kind; and cattle after their kind, and every thing that creepeth upon the earth after his kind; and God saw that it was good. And God said., Let us make man in our image, after our likeness; and let them have dominion over the fish of the sea, and over the fowl of the air, and over the cattle, and over all the earth, and over every creeping thing that

creepeth upon the earth. So God created man in his own image, in the image of God created he him; male and female created he them, And God blessed them, and God said unto them, Be fruitful and multiply, and replenish the earth, and subdue it; and have dominion over the fish of the sea, and over the fowl of the air, and over every living thing that moveth upon the earth. And God said, Behold, I have given you every herb bearing seed, which is upon the face of all the earth, and every tree, in the which is the fruit of a tree yielding seed; to you it shall be for meat, And to every beast of the earth, and to every fowl of the air, and to everything that creepeth upon the earth, wherein there is life*, I have given every green herb for meat; and it was so. And God saw everything that he had made, behold, it was very good. And the evening and morning were the sixth day. (Genesis 1:24–31)

Day 6 is the day for man. Every race was created on day 6. Everything God has accomplished from day 1 to this point was done for man. The moment man's first breath was taken was the culmination of all of God's efforts, every moment prior for six days. Every action was done in love to prepare for man. Nothing was overlooked, and man was not created until man's home was the exact dwelling our Father desired. Six is the number for man. More specifically, 6 denotes the weakness of man, the evils of Satan. Six is the manifestation of sin. Sin is in every man, save one—that is, the Son of Man, Jesus Christ. Before day 6, sin existed in the rebellion of some of the angels and some of God's children. The penalty of treason was going to be paid by God himself, Jesus Christ, allowing man to escape death. It grieved God to make man in the flesh (with sin), but it had to be done because of the war of rebellion (Genesis 6:6). Notice the reference numbers, and this is day 6. God had to teach man the consequences of rebellion in order to bring an end to it. Earth has just been rejuvenated and, in all its beauty, is a battleground. Imagine the love that drives one to make beautiful the very field of battle for the loved one. Nothing is too good for man when seen in the eyes of our Father. In all its beauty, man will find this home to be a temporary residence.

We all know there are ups and downs associated with the lives we are living here on this earth. We know not too much time will pass before we have to endure an attack of the enemy. The truth is, the Lord does not leave us alone to face these attacks. He has promised that he will never leave or forsake us. He keeps his promises.

On day 6, God reminded us of day 1 by making cattle after their kind. The next thing done by God was to show man was in the image of God. Man was made after his kind. We become their kind if we refuse to choose God. Man is made in the image of God and after God's likeness. God owns man. Every emotion experienced by man teaches us God has that same emotion. Man, like God, also has a trinity. Remember 3 means divine completeness and perfection. The number 3 also is the number for resurrection. By making man with a trinity, God was showing man was complete and we are going home after our tour of duty in the flesh bodies. The Trinity of God is the Father, Son, and the Holy Spirit. The trinity of man is the flesh, soul, and the spirit. The Word of God was written by the inspiration of the Holy Spirit. God chose every word and every sentence in the Word of God, leaving nothing unanswered. God chose every word in every sentence structure to provide the specific meaning intended. If anyone ever doubts that every word God chose was chosen to provide a specific meaning in his sentence structure, show that person the following. On day 6, God emphasized the number 3, seven times in the way God chose his words. The number 7 means rest and the completeness of God. First when God said, "Let us make man," he said, "[1] in our image, [2] after our likeness, [3] let them have dominion." When God was calling for man to have dominion, it was dominion over five things: (1) over fish of the sea, (2) over fowl of the air, (3) over the cattle, (4) over all the earth, (5) over every creeping thing that creepeth upon earth.

LOVE IS

Five means grace. As soon as God called for man, the call was in three parts showing man was complete and showing man would be resurrected. God called for man to have power (dominion) over five things showing grace. Every man from the beginning (Jesus) to the end (Jesus) has power over grace. This is to say that every man was made to be resurrected. The power to be resurrected is by grace. God gave every man the power to either accept grace or deny grace.

Part One—Acts
"In the Beginning"
Day Seven

> Thus the heavens and the earth were finished, and all the host of them. And on the seventh day God ended his work which he had made; and be rested on the seventh day from all his work which he had made. And God blessed the seventh day and sanctified it; because that in it he had rested from all his work which God created and made. (Genesis 2:1–3)

On day 7, our Father gave the sweetest gift of all: the gift of rest. It is this gift that allows us to be still with confidence knowing assuredly that we are safe, secure, loved, and protected. We are at rest and find true peace when we deeply plant our roots in Jesus. Faith is the only ingredient required for finding this rest. Jesus is the Word of God, and by planting oneself in him, we find the faith required for acquiring true rest if freely given. It is this seventh day of rest that teaches man that he need not worry or try to reach perfection to gain access to heaven. God was showing man that he wants man with him and provided man the way to heaven through his own beloved Son, Jesus Christ. This gift was not given to man in the spirit of strict law but given in love for man. God was giving man one day in seven a chance to rest and enjoy the fellowship of loved ones. This is a chance to strengthen the family and meet acquaintances new and old. This is a day to enjoy, edify, and share love with others, bringing happiness to the youth and comfort to the seniors. No other gift can compare to the seventh day of rest. This day provides a glimpse into eternity, highlighting the peace, security, and love that is ours to share with our Father. One day in seven feels like heaven already.

With the giving of our precious Savior's blood poured out on the cross, this day is freely given to whomever will to receive. When accepted, this one day in seven becomes every day for those that receive it. We rest in the work that Jesus did for us. We no longer need to prepare ourselves to meet our Creator. All gifts given by God to man are wrapped up in this single day. As this one day shows, the work of God is complete, and he has provided man everything needed for success and eternal happiness shared with him. For God, the seventh day was a day of great joy and happiness. All of God's work in the preparation for man and demonstrating his eternal love and protection with guidance for man was complete. As Jesus turned our one day in seven into every day of rest, so also we can talk with God every day. We need not wait for a special occasion to speak to God. We have access to him at all times.

> And he was teaching in one of the synagogues on the sabbath, And, behold, there was a woman which had a spirit of infirmity eighteen *** years, and was bowed together, and could in no wise lift up herself. And when Jesus saw her, he called her to him, and said unto her, Woman, thou art loosed from thine infirmity. And he laid his hands on her: and immediately she was made straight, and glorified God. And the ruler of the synagogue answered with indignation, because that Jesus had healed on the sabbath day, and said unto the people, There are six days in which men ought to work; in them therefore come and be healed, and not on the sabbath day.
>
> The Lord then answered him, Thou hypocrite, doth not each of you on the sabbath loose his ox or his ass from the stall, and lead him away

to watering? And ought not this woman, being a daughter of Abraham, whom Satan hath bound, lo, these eighteen *** years, be loosed from this bond on the sabbath day? And when he had said these things, all of his adversaries were ashamed: and all the people rejoiced for all the glorious things that were done by him. (Luke 13:10–17)

Jesus teaching on the sabbath (seventh day) was in church, and the lesson taught was, he has the power to free all that are in bondage to Satan. This woman that Jesus healed had an infirmity eighteen years, and 18 is the number meaning bondage. Notice Jesus was in church and it was the ruler of the church taking the occasion to find fault in Jesus. This did happen on this day and has happened a thousand or more times since, but the truth is, Jesus is far greater than any attack made on him by the enemy. We know that Satan will continue to attack our Father and our Savior with no letup. This was spoken of in the Scriptures when the Lord let us know, not only would the attacks continue but would increase. "He that overcometh, the same shall be clothed in white raiment, and I will not blot out his name out of the book of life, but I will confess his name before my Father, and before his angels" (Revelation 3:5).

To recap what we have discussed, it is clear that Jesus is easily seen in each day of creation.

Day One

"I am Alpha and Omega, the beginning and the ending, saith the Lord, which is, and which was, and which is to come, the Almighty" (Revelation 1:8). Jesus is actually the beginning, the ending, and everything in between. All of man's hopes, desires, passion, communion, love, and life itself is centered in Jesus. Without Jesus, there is no life. The first day started with our Father declaring, "Let there be Jesus." Jesus was our Father's answer to the war of rebellion started in eternity past by Satan.

When God divided the light from the darkness, Jesus was the standard that divided the two. Our Father placed the power to win this war in his only begotten Son. Nothing in all our Father's Word can compare to the significance of Jesus. He is the Word.

Day Two

God provided the atmosphere on day 2. This is the air that we breathe. *Soul* (*Nephesh* ["neh'-fesh"] in Hebrew) comes from the root word *Nahfash*, which means to breathe or be breathed upon. Our atmosphere represents the Holy Spirit giving life to all that receive it. The Holy Spirit is often seen as the wind (Genesis 2:7, Ezekiel 37:9–14, and Acts 1:1–8). Jesus is the one that sent the Holy Spirit (John 16:1–7). The purpose of the Holy Spirit is to glorify Jesus (John 16:13–15). The Holy Spirit is the power holding all that come to Jesus sealed in him unto the day of redemption (Ephesians 4:30).

Day Three

Day 3 was the first time we saw the phrase "his kind." As we have already seen, this is a direct reference to Jesus. We also saw the seed of his kind being the seed of Jesus. When God brought forth the dry land, it was the earth being baptized. We learned in the first chapter of John that it was actually Jesus that created all things; therefore, it was Jesus that was baptizing the whole earth on day 3.

Today all that accept Jesus are baptized by the Holy Spirit into the body of Jesus, making us his body (1 Corinthians 12:13). Again, the purpose of the Holy Spirit is to glorify Jesus. Herbs are our Father's prescription for man. Man has used herbs for their medicinal purposes throughout all time. Ancient Chinese writings detail the use of herbs used for medicine dated back as far as before Christ. Jesus is the true herb able to heal man's true disease: rebellion.

LOVE IS

Day Four

We have already seen how the Son can be seen in the sun. The light of the world is the knowledge of the glory of God in the face of Jesus Christ. The sun, moon, and stars are used repeatedly throughout the Word of God as signs of the Second Coming of Jesus. God said the lights of the heavens were to divide the light from the night; this, too, is a direct reference to Jesus. Jesus is the divider (Matthew 25:31–34).

Day Five

Days 1 and 4 showed us that Jesus is the divider. Day 5 shows us what Jesus is dividing. Day 5 was the first time we see the use of both phrases, "his kind" and "their kind." The number 5 means grace. Grace is God's answer to the war and is provided to all his kind through him (Jesus), and we are only his kind by coming to God through Jesus. Day 5 also brought the fowl of the air, and it was the dove (representing the Holy Spirit) landing on Jesus while he was being baptized.

Day Six

Six is the number for man, and Jesus is *the man*. Jesus is the Man that would come with the power to redeem man to God. Jesus is the Son of Man, the perfect man. All men that will live in love with our Father throughout eternity will be alive only in Jesus.

Day Seven

Day 7 gave man rest, and we know that Jesus is the only way to find rest. Only through Jesus are we given the sweetest gift of all: peace and rest. God gave rest in the spirit in which he gave Jesus. That spirit was the spirit of love and not strict law. Jesus can be seen in every day of recreation. Jesus truly is the entire Word of God.

There are, as one might expect, many ways to begin a book. This being the information age, I am sure most of you look at books the way I do; either we are being entertained or we expect information that will make our lives easier. Regardless of the subject being presented, we do expect truth and honesty. If not presented correctly, we may miss out on some very valuable insight as to how we may improve our lives.

This book is presented to you with truth and honor. This is the line in the sand by which the Lord operates. He will offer you nothing less. Have you ever known an honorable man, one who will do nothing that may mar his reputation? To those of us who have difficulty achieving such high standards, it becomes abundantly clear they march by the beat of a different drum. God's honor and truthfulness leave this woman; although to us he seems worlds ahead of us, God's truth and honor can only be realized through God himself.

We can trust what is in the Bible like nothing else we have ever known. There is always a question about worldly wisdom; should we trust or no? It is a total relief to be able to trust what God says. This position can only be reached when listening to the Lord, Jesus Christ. For me, trying to relay truth from God to the reader of this book, it takes me down a path that is easy to tread because of an easiness in relating God's truth.

The next portion of this book will show the relationship among God, the Father, and Jesus Christ, the Son of God, and the Holy Spirit. Without the ability to show their relationship, we are exercising our mental muscles with no future benefit, but being able to show their relationship with each other, we can understand the reality of the Trinity. Once we reach the point of knowledge of the Godhead, it becomes quite easy to give God the place he deserves in each of our lives.

To be totally correct in relating the relationship of the Godhead, I chose to not relate my thoughts and opinions. I chose instead to quote the Bible to lead you to absolute truth.

The next portion of this book will relate to you the connection among God, the Father, and Jesus Christ, the Son of God, and the Holy Spirit.

And God said, Let us make man in our image, after our likeness, and let them have dominion over the fish and over the fowl of the air, and over the cattle, and all the earth, and over every creeping thing that creepeth upon the earth.

So God created man in his own image, in the image of God created he him; male and female created he them.

And God blessed them, and God said unto them, Be fruitful and multiply, and replenish the earth, and subdue it; and have dominion over the fish of the sea, and over the fowl of the air, and over every living thing that moveth upon the earth. (Genesis 1:26–28)

And now, O Father, glorify thou me with thine own self with the glory which I had with thee before the world was. (John 17:5)

O Righteous Father, the world hath not known thee; but I have known thee, and these have known that thou hast sent me. (John 17:25)

For God so loved the world, that he gave his only begotten Son, that whosoever believeth in him should not perish, but have everlasting life.

For God sent not his Son into the world to condemn the world; but that the world through him might be saved.

He that believeth on him is not condemned; but he that believeth not is condemned already, because he hath not believed in the name of the only begotten Son of God. (John 3:16–18)

In the beginning was the Word, and the Word was with God, and the Word was God.

The same was in the beginning with God.

All things were made by him; and without him was not anything made that was made.

In him was life; and the life was the light of men. (John 1:1–4)

But as many as received him, to them gave the power to become sons of God, even to them that believe on his name.

Which were born, not of blood, nor of the will of the flesh, nor of the will of man, but of God. 14 And the Word was made flesh, and dwelt among us, (And we beheld his glory, the glory as of the only begotten of the Father) full of grace and truth. (John 1:12–13)

For the law was given by Moses, but grace and truth came by Jesus Christ.

No man hath seen God at any time; the only begotten Son, which is in the bosom of the Father, he hath declared him. (John 1:17–18)

The thief cometh not, but for to steal, and to kill, and to destroy; I am come that they might have life, and that they might have it more abundantly.

I am the good shepherd; the good shepherd giveth his life for the sheep. (John 10:10–11)

As the Father knoweth me, even so know I the Father; and I lay down my life for the sheep. 17 Therefore doth my Father love me, because I lay down my life, that I might take it again. (John 10:15)

No man taketh it from me, but I lay it down of myself. I have power to lay it down, and I have power to take it again. This commandment have I received of my Father. (John 10:18)

Jesus saith unto him, I am the way, the truth, and the life; no man cometh unto the Father, but by me. (John 14:6)

Believest thou not that I am in the Father, and the Father is in me? The words that I speak unto you I speak not of myself; but the Father that dwelleth in me, he doeth the works. (John 14:10)

These things have I spoken unto you, being yet present with you.
But the Comforter, which is the Holy Ghost, whom the Father will send in my name, he shall teach you all things, and bring all things to your remembrance, whatsoever I have said unto you.
Peace I leave with you, my peace I give unto you: not as the world giveth, give I unto you, Let not your heart be troubled, neither let it be afraid.
You have heard how I said unto you, I go away, and come again unto you. If ye loved me, you would rejoice, because I said, I go into the Father: for my Father is greater than I.
And now I have told you before it come to pass, that, when it is come to pass, ye might believe. (John 14:25–29)

Nevertheless I tell you the truth. It is expedient for you that I go away; the Comforter will not come unto you; but if I depart; I will send him unto you. (John 16:7)

Howbeit when he, the Spirit of Truth is come, he will guide you into all truth; for he shall not speak of himself, but whatsoever he shall hear, that shall he speak; and he will show you things to come. (John 16:13)

And this is life eternal, that they might know thee, the only true God, and Jesus Christ, whom thou hast sent. (John 17:3)

Now they have known that all things whatsoever thou hast given me are of thee.
For I have given unto them the words which thou gavest me, and they have received them, and have known surely that I came out from thee, and they have believed that thou didst send me.
I pray for them: I pray not for the world, but for them which thou hast given me, for they are thine. (John 17:7–9)

Neither pray I for these alone, but for them also which shall believe on me through their word.
That they all may be one, as thou, Father, art in me, and I in thee, that they also may be one in us; that the world may believe that thou hast sent me. (John 17:20–21)

As birds flying, so will the Lord of hosts defend Jerusalem: defending also he will deliver it: and passing over he will preserve it. (Isaiah 31:5)

LOVE IS

For the Lord is our judge, the Lord is our lawgiver, the Lord is our king, he will save us. (Isaiah 33:22)

The grass withereth, the flower fadeth; but the word of our God shall stand forever. (Isaiah 40:8)

I will say to the north, Give up; and to the south, Keep not back; bring my sons from far, and my daughters from the ends of the earth.
Even everyone that is called by my name; for I have created him for my glory, I have formed him; yea, I have made him. (Isaiah 43:6–7)

Ye are my witnesses, saith the Lord, and my servant whom I have chosen. That ye may know and believe me and understand that I am he: before me there was no God formed, neither shall there be after me.
I, even I, am the Lord; and beside me there is no savior.
I have declared, and have saved, and I have shewed, when there was no strange god among you; therefore ye are my witnesses, saith the Lord, that I am God. (Isaiah 43:10–12)

I will go before thee, and make the crooked places straight; I will break in pieces the gates of brass, and cut in sunder the bars of iron;
And I will give thee the treasures of darkness, and hidden riches of secret places, that thou mayest know that I, the Lord, which call thee by name, am the God of Israel. (Isaiah 45:2–3)

I am the Lord, and there is none else, there is no God beside me; I girded thee, though thou hast not known me.

That they may know from the rising of the sun, and from the west, that there is none beside me, I am the Lord, and there is none else.

I form the light, and create darkness: I make peace, and create evil: I the Lord do all these things. (Isaiah 45:5–7)

Therefore my people shall know my name: therefore they shall know in that day that I am he that doth speak: behold, it is I. (Isaiah 52:6)

And all thy children shall be taught of the Lord; and great shall be the peace of thy children. (Isaiah 54:13)

For since the beginning of the world men have not heard, nor perceived by the ear, neither hath the eye seen, O God, beside thee, what he hath prepared for him that waiteth for him. (Isaiah 65:4)

But we see Jesus, who was made a little lower than the angels for the suffering of death, crowned with glory and honor; that he by the grace of God should taste death for every man.

For it became him, for whom are all things, and by whom are all things, in bringing many sons into glory, to make the captain of their salvation perfect through sufferings. (Hebrews 2:9–10)

Forasmuch then as the children are partakers of flesh and blood, he also himself likewise took part of the same: that through death he might destroy him that had the power of death, that is, the devil.

And deliver them who through fear of death were all their lifetime subject to bondage. (Hebrews 2:14–15)

For the word of God is quick and powerful and sharper than any two-edged sword, piercing even to the dividing asunder of soul and spirit, and of the joints and marrow, and is a discerner of the thoughts and intents of the heart.

Neither is there any creature that is not manifest in his sight; but all things are naked and opened unto the eyes of him with whom we have to do.

Seeing then that we have a great high priest, that is passed into the heavens, Jesus the Son of God, let us hold fast our profession.

For we have not an high priest which cannot be touched with the feeling of our infirmities; but was in all points tempted like as we are, yet without sin.

Let us therefore come boldly unto the throne of grace, that we may obtain mercy, and find grace to help in time of need. (Hebrews 4:12–16)

So also Christ glorified not himself to be made an high priest; but he that said unto him, Thou art my son, today have I begotten thee.

As he saith also in another place, Thou art a priest for ever after the order of Mel-chis-e-dec.

Who in the days of his flesh, when he had offered up prayers and supplications with strong crying and tears unto him that was able to save him from death and was heard in that he feared.

Though he were a son, yet learned he obedience by the things which he suffered.

And being made perfect, he became the author of eternal salvation unto all them that obey him. (Hebrews 5:5–9)

For he hath made him to be sin for us, who knew no sin, that we might be made the righteousness of God in him. (2 Corinthians 5:21)

Therefore if any man be in Christ, he is a new creature, old things are passed away; behold all things are become new. (2 Corinthians 5:17)

For he saith, I have heard thee in a time accepted, and in the day of salvation have I succored thee; behold now is the accepted time; behold now is the day of salvation. (2 Corinthians 6:2)

Now the birth of Jesus Christ was on this wise; When as his mother Mary was espoused to Joseph, before they came together, she was found with child of the Holy Ghost.

Then Joseph her husband, being a just man, and not willing to make her a Publick example, was minded to put her away privily.

But while he thought on these things, behold, the angel of the Lord appeared unto him in a dream, saying, Joseph, thou son of David, fear not to take unto thee Mary thy wife: for that which is conceived in her is of the Holy Ghost.

And she shall bring forth a son, and thou shalt call his name Jesus: for he shall save his people from their sins.

Now all this was done, that it might be fulfilled which was spoken of the Lord by the prophet saying,

Behold a virgin shall be with child, and shall bring forth a son, and they shall call his name Emman-uel, which being interpreted is, God with us.

Then Joseph, being raised from sleep did as the angel of the Lord had bidden him, and took unto him his wife.

And knew her not till she had brought forth her firstborn son: and he called his name Jesus. (Matthew 1:18–25)

I indeed baptize you with water unto repentance: but he that cometh after me is mightier than I, whose shoes I am not worthy to bear; he shall baptize you with the Holy Ghost, and with fire. (Matthew 3:11)

And Jesus, when he was baptized, went straightway out of the water; and lo, the heavens were opened unto him, and he saw, the spirit of God descending like a dove, and lighting upon him.

And lo, a voice from heaven, saying, This is my beloved Son, in whom I am well pleased. (Matthew 3:16–17)

But, he held his peace, and answered nothing, Again, the high priest asked him, and said unto him, art thou the Christ, the Son of the Blessed?

And Jesus said, I am; and ye shall see the Son of man sitting on the right hand of power, and coming in the clouds of Heaven. (Mark 14:61–62)

Behold I give unto you power to tread on serpents and scorpions, and over all the power of the enemy; and nothing shall by any means hurt you. (Luke 10:19)

And behold a certain lawyer stood up, and tempted him, saying, Master, what shall I do to inherit eternal life?
He said unto him, What is written in the law? How readest thou?
And he answering said, Thou shalt love the Lord thy God with all thy heart, and with all thy soul, and with all thy strength, and with all thy mind, and thy neighbor as thyself. (Luke 10:25–27)

Also I say unto you, whosoever shall confess me before men, him shall the Son of man also confess before the angels of God.
But he that denieth me before men shall be denied before the angels of God.
And whosoever shall speak a word against the Son of man, it shall be forgiven him; but unto him that blasphemeth against the Holy Ghost it shall not be forgiven. (Luke 112:8–10)

Stand fast therefore in the liberty wherewith Christ hath made us free, and be not entangled again with the yoke of bondage. (Galatians 5:1)

For, brethren, ye have been called into liberty; only use not liberty for an occasion to the flesh, but by love serve one another. (Galatians 5:13)

Be not deceived, God is not mocked; for whatsoever a man soweth, that so he shall also reap.

For he that soweth to his flesh shall of the flesh reap corruption: but he that soweth to the Spirit shall of the Spirit reap life everlasting. (Galatians 6:7–8)

And grieve not the Holy Spirit of God, whereby ye are sealed unto the day of redemption. (Ephesians 4:30)

Whereof, I was made a minister, according to the gift of the grace of God given unto me by the effectual working of his power.

Unto me, who am less of all saints, is this grace given, that I should preach among the gentiles the unsearchable riches of Christ.

And to make all men see what is the fellowship of the mystery, which from the beginning of the world hath been hid in God, who created all things by Jesus Christ.

To the intent that now unto the principalities and powers in heavenly places might be known by the church, the manifold wisdom of God.

According to the eternal purpose which he purposed in Christ Jesus our Lord. In whom we have boldness and access with confidence by the faith of him.

Wherefore, I desire that you faint not at my tribulations for you, which is your glory.

For this cause I bow my knees to the Father of our Lord Jesus Christ.

Of whom the whole family in heaven and earth is named. (Ephesians 3:7–15)

Being confident of this very thing, that he which hath begun a good work in you will perform it until the day of Jesus Christ. (Philippians 1:6)

For to me to live is Jesus Christ and to die is gain. (Philippians 1:21)

Only let your conversation be as it becometh the gospel of Christ. (Philippians 1:27)

For it is God which worketh in you both to will and to do of his good pleasure.

Do all things without murmurings and disputing's.

Let us therefore, as many as be perfect, be thus minded; and if anything you be otherwise minded, God shall reveal even this to you. (Philippians 2:13–15)

Be careful for nothing; but in everything by prayer and supplication with thanksgiving let your requests be made known unto God.

And the peace of God, which passeth all understanding shall keep your hearts and minds through Christ Jesus. (Philippians 4:6–7)

For he taught his disciples and said unto them; The Son of man is delivered unto the hands of men, and they shall kill him; and after that he is killed, he shall rise the third day. (Mark 9:31)

For even the Son of man came not to be ministered unto, but to minister, and to give his life a ransom for many. (Mark 10:45)

The next day John, (the Baptist) seeth Jesus coming unto him, and saith, Behold the Lamb of God, which taketh away the sin of the world.
This is he of whom I said, After me cometh a man which is preferred before me; for he was before me.
And I knew him not; but that he should be made manifest to Israel, therefore am I come baptizing with water.
And John bare record, saying I saw the Spirit descending from heaven like a dove, and it abode upon him.
And I knew him not, but he that sent me to baptize with water, the same said unto me, Upon whom thou shalt see the Spirit descending, and remaining on him, the same is he which baptizeth with the Holy Ghost.
And I saw and bare record that this is the Son of God. (John 1:29–34)

For as much as you know that ye were not redeemed with corruptible things, as silver and gold, from your vain conversation received by tradition from your fathers.
But with the precious blood of Christ, as of a lamb without blemish and without spot.

Who verily was foreordained before the foundation of the world but was manifest in these last times for you. (1 Peter 1:18–20)

And they overcame him by the blood of the Lamb, and by the word of their testimony; and they loved not their lives unto the death.

Therefore, rejoice ye heavens and ye that dwell in them. Woe to the inhabitants of the earth and of the sea; for the devil is come down unto you, having great wrath, because he knoweth he hath but a short time. (Revelation 12:11–12)

The Third Person of the Trinity, the Holy Spirit

For as many as were led by the Spirit of God, they are the Sons of God.

For you have not received the Spirit of bondage again to fear; but you have received the Spirit of adoption, whereby we cry Ab-ba Father.

The Spirit itself beareth witness With our spirit, that we are the children of God.

And if children, then heirs; heirs of God, and joint heirs with Christ; if so be that we suffer with him, that we may be also glorified together.

For I reckon that the sufferings of this present time are not worthy to be compared with the glory which shall be revealed in us. (Romans 8:14–18)

The Holy Spirit, being the third person of the Trinity, will teach us all things, whatsoever Jesus says and will bring to remembrance all things.

Likewise the Spirit also helpeth our infirmities: for we know not what we should pray for as we ought: but the Spirit itself maketh intercession for us with groanings which cannot be uttered.

And he that searcheth the hearts knoweth what is the mind of the Spirit, because he maketh intercession for the Saints according to the will of God.

And we know that all things work together for good to them that love God, to them who are the called according to his purpose.

For whom he did foreknow, he also did predestinate to be conformed to the image of his Son, that he might be the first born among many brethren. (Romans 8:26–29)

But ye, beloved, building up yourselves on your most holy faith, praying in the Holy Ghost.

Keep yourselves in the love of God, looking for the mercy of our Lord Jesus Christ unto eternal life.

And of some have compassion, making a difference.

And others, save with fear, pulling them out of the fire: hating even the garment spotted by the flesh.

Now unto him that is able to keep you from falling, and to present you faultless before the presence of his glory with exceeding joy.

To the only wise God, our Savior, be glory and majesty, dominion and power, both now and ever. A-men. (Jude 1:20–25)

God is with thee in all that thou doest. (Genesis 21:22)

Thou shalt not take the name of the Lord thy God in vain; for the Lord will not hold him guiltless that taketh his name in vain. (Deuteronomy 5:11)

And thou shalt love the Lord thy God with all thine heart, and with all thy soul, and with all thy might.

And these words, which I command thee this day, shall be in thine heart. (Deuteronomy 6:5–6)

Know therefore that the Lord thy God, he is God, the faithful God, which keepeth covenant and mercy with them that love him and keep his commandments to a thousand generations.

And repayeth them that hate him to their face, to destroy them; he will not be slack to him that hateth him, he will repay him to his face. (Deuteronomy 7:9–10)

But thou shalt remember the Lord thy God: for it is he that giveth thee power to get wealth, that he may establish his covenant which he swore unto thy fathers, as it is this day. (Deuteronomy 8:18)

When the Lord shall build up Zion, he shall appear in his glory.

He will regard the prayer of the destitute, and not despise their prayer.

This shall be written for the generation to come; and the people which shall be created shall praise the Lord.

For he hath looked down from the height of his sanctuary from heaven did the Lord behold the earth.

To hear the groaning of the prisoner: to loose those that are appointed to death.

To declare the name of the Lord in Zion, and his praise in Jerusalem. (Psalm 102:16–21)

But God, who is rich in mercy, for his great love wherewith he loved us.

Even when we were dead in sins, quickened us together with Christ (by grace you are saved)

And hath raised us up together, and made us sit together in heavenly places in Christ Jesus.

That in the ages to come he might shew the exceeding riches of his grace in his kindness toward us through Christ Jesus, for by grace are you saved through faith; and that not of yourselves; it is the gift of God. (Ephesians 2:4–7)

Do we then make void the law through faith? God forbid; yea, we establish the law. (Romans 3:31)

For what saith the scripture? Abraham believed God, and it was counted unto him for righteousness. (Romans 4:3)

Saying, Blessed are they whose iniquities are forgiven, and whose sins are covered.

Blessed is the man to whom the Lord will not impute sin. (Romans 4:7–8)

He staggered not at the promise of God through unbelief, but was strong in faith, giving glory to God.

And being fully persuaded that, what he had promised, he was able also to perform.

And therefore it was imputed to him for righteousness. (Romans 4:20–22)

Now it was not written for his sake alone, that it was imputed to him.

But for us also, to whom it shall be imputed, if we believe on him that raised up Jesus, our Lord from the dead

Who was delivered for our offences, and was raised again for our justifications. (Romans 4:23–25)

Men's hearts failing them for fear, and for looking after those things which are coming on the earth: for the powers of heaven shall be shaken.

And then shall they see the Son of Man coming in a cloud with power and great glory.

And when these things begin to come to pass; then look up and lift up your heads, for your redemption draweth nigh. (Luke 21:26–28)

And this gospel of the kingdom shall be preached in all the world for a witness unto all nations; and then shall the end come. (Matthew 24:14)

For there shall arise false Christs, and false prophets, and shall show great signs and wonders: insomuch that, if it were possible, they shall deceive the very elect. (Matthew 24:24)

And Jesus answered and said unto them, Take heed that no man deceive you.

For many shall come in my name, saying, I am Christ: and shall deceive many.

And ye shall hear of wars and rumors of wars; see that ye be not troubled: for all these things must come to pass, but the end is not yet.

For nation shall rise against nation, and kingdom against kingdom: and there shall be famines, and pestilences, and earthquakes, in divers places.

All these are the beginning of sorrows. (Matthew 24:4–8)

For this we say unto you by the word of the Lord, that we which are alive and remain unto the coming of the Lord shall not prevent them which are asleep.

For the Lord himself shall descend from heaven with a shout, with the trump of God: and the dead in Christ shall rise first.

Then we which are alive and remain shall be caught up together with them in the clouds, to meet the Lord in he air, and so shall we ever be with the Lord. (1 Thess. 4:15–17)

Let not your bean be troubled; ye believe in God, believe also in me.

In my Fathers' house are many mansions: if it were not so, I would have told you; I go to prepare a place for you.

And if I go and prepare a place for you, I will come again, and receive you unto myself; that where I am, there ye may be also. (John 14:1–3)

Jesus saith unto him, I am the way, the truth, and the life; no man cometh to the Father but by me. (John 14:6)

How shall we escape, if we neglect so great salvation; which at the first began to be spoken by the Lord, and was confirmed unto us by them that heard him.

God also bearing them witness, both with signs and wonders, and with divers miracles, and gifts of the Holy Ghost, according to his own will. (Hebrews 2:3–4)

Your words have been stout against me, saith the Lord. Yet ye say, What have we spoken so much against thee?

Ye have said, It is vain to serve God, and what profit is it that we have kept his ordinance, and that we have walked mournfully before the Lord of Hosts

And now we call the proud happy, yea, they that work wickedness are set up; yea, they that tempt God are even delivered.

Then they that feared the Lord spoke often one to another; and the Lord hearkened, and heard it, and a book of remembrance was written before him for them that feared the Lord, and that thought upon his name.

And they shall be mine, saith the Lord of Hosts, In that day when I make up my jewels, and I will spare them as a man spareth his own son, that serveth him…

Then shall ye return, and discern between the righteous and the wicked, between him that serveth God and him that serveth him not. (Malachi 3:13–18)

For, behold, the day cometh, that shall bum as an oven, and all the proud, yea, and all that do wickedly, shall be stubble, and the day that cometh shall bum them up, saith the Lord of Hosts that it shall leave them neither root nor branch.

But unto you that fear my name, shall the Sun of righteousness arise with healing in his wings; and ye shall go forth, and grow up as calves of the stall.

And ye shall tread down the wicked; for they shall be ashes under the soles of your feet, in the day that I shall do this, saith the Lord of Hosts. (Malachi 4:1–3)

And God said, Let us make man in our image, after our likeness, and let them have dominion over the fish and over the fowl of the air, and over the cattle, and all the earth, and over every creeping thing that creeps upon the earth. So GOD CREATED MAN IN HIS OWN IMAGE, in the image of God created he him; male and female, created he them.
And God blessed them, and God said unto them, Be fruitful and multiply, and replenish the earth, and subdue it, and have dominion over the fish of the sea, and over the fowl of the air, and over every living thing that moves upon the earth. (Genesis 1:26–28)

And now, O Father, glorify thou me with thy own self with the glory which I had with thee before the world was. (John 17:5)

O righteous Father, the world hath not known thee; and these have known that thou has sent me. (John 17:25)

For God so loved the world, that he gave his only begotten Son, that whosoever believes in him should not perish, but have everlasting life.
For God sent not his son into the world to condemn the world, but that the world through him might be saved.
He that believes on him is not condemned; but he that believes not is condemned already.

Because he has not believed in the only begotten Son of God. (John 3:16–18)

In the beginning was the Word, and the Word was with God, and the Word was God. The same was in the beginning with God.

All things were made by him; and without him was not anything made that was made.

In him was life; and the life was the light of men. (John 1:1–4)

But as many as received him, to them gave he power to become sons of God, even to them that believed on his name. (John 1:12)

Anointing

> Those that be planted in the House of the Lord shall flourish in the courts of our God.
>
> They shall still bring forth fruit in old age; they shall be fat and flourishing.
>
> Every word you say will come to pass if you are full of righteousness in the anointing. Spiritual maturity lines up with decisions made on the word of God. This has nothing to do with the length of time being saved. (Psalm 92:13–14)

> I give unto you power to tread on serpents and scorpions, and over all power of the enemy; and nothing shall by any means hurt you. (Luke 10:19)

Power has a name. That name is Jesus.

We are anointed to win every time. God gives the ability to do whatever he wants us to do. When he positions us to do the work that he has called us to do, he gives us the ability to do whatever that may be.

Restoration comes when the anointing comes. He will restore unto us what the enemy has stolen from us. I am anointed. I am what God says I am. I have what God says I have.

> Now when all the people were baptized, it came to pass, that Jesus also being baptized, and praying, the Heaven was opened.

> And the Holy Ghost descended in a bodily shape like a dove upon him, and a voice from heaven, which said, thou art my beloved Son; in thee I am well pleased. (Luke 3:21–22)

Nothing gets accomplished without the anointing.

And it shall come to pass in the day that his burden shall be taken away from off thy shoulder and his yoke from off thy neck, and the yoke shall be destroyed because of the anointing.

The anointing destroys yokes. The anointing will cause success while removing burdens. No burden can defeat the anointing. The anointing removes depression. Yield to the anointing. Line up your thinking with the anointing.

> But strong meat belongeth to them that are of full age, even those who by reason of use have their senses exercised to discern both good and evil.
>
> The anointing is for service or mission. Thy throne, O God is for ever and ever; the scepter of thy kingdom is a right scepter. (Hebrews 5:14)
>
> Thou lovest righteousness, and hatest wickedness; therefore God, thy God hath anointed thee with the oil of gladness above thy fellows.
>
> Jesus loves righteousness and hates wickedness. (Psalm 45:7)

> For he hath made him to be sin for us, who knew no sin; that we might be made the righteousness of God in him.
>
> The anointing will grow as righteousness grows. (2 Corinthians 5:21)

Supernatural increase happens to anointed people.

Blood of Jesus

We plead the blood over everything in our lives. The Father gave us his Son. What, therefore, is there that he would not do for us? Will he not heal us or take care of us? Whosoever will honor the blood of Jesus will in turn receive honor from the Father. The blood of Jesus will heal all, cure all, eagerly take care of all our problems.

When Jesus died on the cross, he redeemed us from the curse of the law.

God's favor rests on those who honor the Son's blood that was shed for us.

Power in the blood of Jesus is the ability to get things done, such as power to release you from every attack of Satan. There is also power to release you from every stronghold of the enemy.

The power to protect you from every onslaught of the devil is in the blood of Jesus.

> For the weapons of our warfare are not carnal, but mighty through God to the pulling down of strongholds. (2 Corinthians 10:4)

> There hath no temptation taken you but such as is common to man, but God is faithful, who will not suffer you to be tempted above that ye are able; but will with the temptation also make a way to escape, that you may be able to bear it.
>
> Therefore my dearly beloved, flee from idolatry.
>
> I speak as to wise men; judge you what I say.

The cup of blessing which we bless; is it not the communion of the blood of Christ? The bread which we break, is it not the communion of the body of Christ.

For we being many are one bread, and one body; for we are all partakers of that one bread. (1 Corinthians 10:13–17)

The Presence of God

> He that dwelleth in the secret place of the most High shall abide under the shadow of the Almighty.
> I will say of the Lord, he is my refuge and my fortress; my God; in him will I trust.
> Surely he shall deliver thee from the snare of the fowler, and from the noisome pestilence.
> He shall cover thee with his feathers, under his wings shalt thou trust; his truth shall be thy shield and buckler. (Psalm 91:1–4)

The Holy Spirit makes things plain.

> In whom you also trusted, after that ye heard, the word of truth, the gospel of your salvation; in whom also after that ye believed, Ye were sealed with that holy Spirit of promise. (Ephesians 1:13)

> For God sent not his Son into the world to condemn the world; but that the world through him might be saved.
> He that believeth on him is not condemned; but he that believeth not is condemned already, because he hath not believed in the name of the only begotten Son of God. (John 3:17–18)

Wherefore I give you to understand, that no man speaking by the Spirit of God calleth Jesus accursed; and that no man can say that Jesus is the Lord, but by the Holy Ghost. (1 Corinthians 12:3)

That Christ may dwell in your hearts by faith; that ye, being rooted and grounded in love.
May be able to comprehend with all saints, what is the breadth and length, and depth, and height: And to know the love of Christ, which passeth knowledge, that ye might be filled with all the fullness of God.
Now unto him that is able to do exceeding abundantly above all that we ask or think, according to the power that worketh in us.
Unto him be glory in the church by Christ Jesus throughout all ages, world without end. A-men. (Ephesians 3:17–21)

You can have confidence to come into the presence of Christ by his blood and body that he gave on the cross.

Thou will show me the path of life; in thy presence is fullness of joy: at thy right hand are pleasures for evermore. (Psalm 16:11)

Surely the righteous shall give thanks unto your name. The upright shall dwell in thy presence. You will do one of two things, either be thankful or complain. You choose. (Psalm 140:13)

For the Lord God is a sun and shield; The Lord will give grace and glory; No good thing

will he withhold from them that walk uprightly.
(Psalm 84:11)

The devil is defeated in the presence of the Lord.

[The Lord speaking to Moses] And he said, My presence shall go with thee, and I will give thee rest. (Exodus 33:14)

Cast your care on Jesus because he cares for you. When you hold care, you are saying you don't trust God.

God is love. Love is the anointing to prosper. Walking in the presence of God is the most significant thing you can do.

The peace of God that passes all understanding comes in his presence.

Cast your care on God. Do not carry the care of the church. The secret place of the Most High is my refuge, my fortress, and my hiding place.

People will know us by the aura we have on us.

Be ye therefore followers of Christ, as dear children. In his presence is fullness of joy. (Ephesians 5:1)

Speak it; say, "I believe, I receive."

Abide in the presence of God. There is peace in his presence. You can't carry depression and peace at the same time; choose peace. It is a choice we make.

Concerning Joseph, the Lord made all that he did to prosper in his hand. (Genesis 39:1)

Preserve me, O God: for in thee do I put my trust. (Psalm 16:1)

The Lord is the portion of my inheritance and of my cup; thou maintainest my lot. (Psalm 16:5)

I have set the Lord always before me; because he is at my right hand, I shall not be moved.
Therefore, my heart is glad, and my glory rejoiceth: my flesh also shall rest in hope.
For thou will not leave my soul in hell; Neither wilt thou suffer thine Holy One to see corruption.
Thou wilt shew me the path of life; in thy presence is fullness of joy; at thy right hand there are pleasures for evermore. (Psalm 16:8–11)

Blessed are they that dwell in thy house; they will be still praising thee. (Psalm 84:4)

Offer unto God thanksgiving; and pay thy vows unto the Most High.
And call upon me in the day of trouble; I will deliver thee, and thou shalt glorify me. (Psalm 50:14–15)

Why Jesus

Why do people gravitate toward Jesus? Why do so many people need Jesus to complete the destiny that they are sure is out there for them? Questions that need an answer, we could go forward and ignore this one. Who has time for this? Why dig deep into something that we have never bothered to look into? Well, I like the way John Doe behaves, I like the way Jane Doe presents herself, so I should present myself in the same manner. Why dig so deep on which way I should go? The truth is, it makes a huge difference in the way I go. It is a matter of whether I go to heaven when I die or go to hell.

No one likes to talk about hell. No one likes to admit they could possibly be wrong about what their beliefs are. This is where most of our arguments come from, a difference of opinion, and of course, my opinion has to be the right one. How could I be wrong? What would happen if I admitted that I was the one who was at fault here?

Just for the sake of argument, let us look into why people choose Jesus to worship. Why choose to follow Christ through this life? Why choose a Savior that gave his life for us instead of us giving our lives for him?

Let's look into this position. Let us soberly and thoughtfully see where this position will lead us. If by looking into why Jesus and no decision can be made as to why we should follow Jesus Christ, then you are free to follow whomever. This is your decision; this is your life. No one can make that decision for you. Now, let's begin a journey leading us to answer the question, "Why Jesus?"

When digging into information concerning "Why Jesus?" we have to infuse what we already know about him with what the Bible tells us. From the very beginning of the Word of God, we see Jesus being brought to the forefront.

In Genesis, we find Jesus there in the beginning. To confirm this, John 1:1–12 says, "In the beginning was the Word, and the Word was with God, and the word was God. The same was in the beginning with God. All things were made by him: and without him was not anything made that was made. In him was life; and the life was the light of men. And the light shineth in darkness; and the darkness comprehended it not. There was a man sent from God, whose name was John. The same came for a witness, to bear witness of the Light, that all men through him might believe. He was not that Light but was sent to bear witness of that Light. That was the true Light, which lighteth every man that cometh into the world. He was in the world, and the world was made by him, and the world knew him not. He came into his own, and his own received him not. But as many as received him, to them gave the power to become the sons of God. Even to them that believe on his name."

Then in verse 17, we read, "For the law was given by Moses, but grace and truth came by Jesus Christ."

Jesus can be found throughout the entire Bible, for there never was a time when Jesus was not.

Now I present to you names and titles that apply to Jesus that are found in the Holy Bible:

- Adam

    And so it is written, The first man Adam was made a living soul; the last Adam was made a quickening spirit. (1 Corinthians 15:45)

- Advocate

    My little children, these things write I unto you, that ye sin not. And if any man sin, we have an advocate with the Father, Jesus Christ the righteous. (1 John 2:1)

- Almighty

    I am Alpha and Omega, the beginning and the ending, saith the Lord, which is, and which was, and which was to come, the Almighty. (Revelation 1:8)

- Amen

    And unto the angel of the church of the La-od-i-ce-ans write; These things saith the Amen, the faithful and true witness, the beginning of the creation of God. (Revelation 3:14)

- Apostle of Our Profession

    Wherefore holy brethren, partakers of the heavenly calling, consider the Apostle and High Priest of our profession, Christ Jesus. (Hebrews 3:1)

- Arm of the Lord

    Who hath believed our report? And to whom is the arm of the Lord revealed? (Isaiah 53:1)

- Author and Finisher of Our Faith

    Looking unto Jesus the author and finisher of our faith, who for the joy that was set before him endured the cross, despising the shame, and is set down at the right hand of the throne of God. (Hebrews 12:2)

LOVE IS

- Author of Our Salvation

    And being made perfect, he became the author of eternal salvation unto all them that obey him. (Hebrews 5:9)

- Beloved Son

    Behold my servant, whom I have chosen, my beloved, in whom my soul is well pleased. (Matthew 12:18)

- Blessed and Only Potentate (one who possesses great power)

    Which in his times he shall shew, who is the blessed and only Potentate, the King of Kings, and Lord of Lords. (1 Timothy 6:15)

- Branch

    In that day shall the branch of the Lord be beautiful and glorious, and the fruit of the earth be excellent and comely for them that are escaped of Israel. (Isaiah 4:2)

    And there shall come forth a rod out of the stem of Jesse, and a branch shall grow out of his roots. (Isaiah 11:1)

- Bread of Life

    Then Jesus said unto them, Verily Verily I say unto you, Moses gave you not that bread from heaven; but, my Father giveth you the true bread from heaven, For the bread of God is he which cometh down from heaven, and giveth life unto the world. Then said they unto him, Lord, evermore give us this bread. And Jesus said unto them I am the bread of life, he that cometh to me shall never hunger. And he that believeth on me shall never thirst. (John 6:32–35)

- Captain of Our Salvation

    For it became him, for whom are all things, and by whom are all things, in bringing many sons unto glory, to make the captain of their salvation perfect through sufferings. (Hebrews 2:10)

- Chief Shepherd

    And when the chief shepherd shall appear, ye shall receive a crown of glory that fadeth not away. (1 Peter 5:4)

- Christ of God (Christ = Anointed)

    He said unto them, "But whom say ye that I am?" Peter answering said, The Christ of God. (Luke 9:20)

- Consolation of Israel

    And, behold, there was a man in Jerusalem whose name was Simeon; and the same man was just and devout, waiting for the consolation of Israel, and the Holy Ghost was upon him. (Luke 2:25)

- Corner Stone

    The stone which the builders refused is become the head stone of the comer. (Psalm 118:22)

    Jesus saith unto them, "Did ye never read in the scriptures, The stone which the builders rejected, the same is become the head of the comer: this is the Lords' doing, and it is marvelous in our eyes?" (Matthew 21:42)

    This is the stone which was set at naught of you builders; which is become the head of the comer. (Acts 4:11)

    And are built upon the foundation of the apostles and prophets, Jesus Christ himself being the chief corner stone. (Ephesians 2:20)

    Wherefore also it is contained in the scripture, Behold I lay in Sion, a chief corner stone, elect, precious, and he that believeth on him shall not be confounded. (1 Peter 2:6)

- Counselor

    For unto us a child is born unto us a son is given: and the government shall be upon his shoulder; and his name shall be called Wonderful, Counselor, The mighty God, The everlasting Father, The prince of Peace. (Isaiah 9:6)

- Creator

    All things were made by him; and without him was not anything made that was made. (John 1:3)

- Dayspring

    Through the tender mercy of our God; whereby the dayspring from on high hath visited us. (Luke 1:78)

- Daystar

    We have also a more sure word of prophecy; whereunto ye do well that ye take heed; as unto a light that shineth in a dark place, until the day dawn, and the day star arise in your hearts. (2 Peter 1:19)

- Deliverer

    And so all Israel shall be saved: as it is written, There shall come out of Sion the Deliverer, and shall turn away ungodliness from Jacob. (Romans 11:26)

- Desired of All Nations

    And I will shake all nations, and the desire of all nations shall come, and I will fill this house with glory; saith the Lord of hosts. (Haggai 2:7)

- Divider

    Think not that I am come to send peace on earth; I came not to send peace but a sword;
    For I am come to set a man at variance against his father, and the daughter against her mother, and the daughter-in-law against her mother-in-law.
    And a mans foes shall be those of his own household.
    He that loveth father or mother more than me is not worthy of me; and he that loveth son or daughter more than me is not worthy of me. (Matthew 10:34–37)

- Door

    Then said Jesus unto them again, "Verily, Verily, I say unto you, I am the door of the sheep." (John 10:7)

- Eagle

    Ye have seen what I did unto the Egyptians, and how I bare you on eagles wings, and brought you unto myself. (Exodus 19:4)

    As an eagle stirreth up her nest, fluttereth over her young, spreadeth abroad her wings, taketh them, beareth them on her wings.
    So the Lord alone did lead him, and there was no strange god with him. (Deuteronomy 32:11–12)

- Elect of God

    Behold, my servant, whom I uphold, mine elect, in whom my soul delighteth; I have put my spirit upon him; he shall bring forth judgment to the Gentiles. (Isaiah 42:1)

- Everlasting Father

    For unto us a child is born, unto us a son is given; and the government shall be upon his shoulder; and his name shall be called Wonderful, Counselor, The mighty God, The everlasting Father, The Prince of Peace. (Isaiah 9:6)

The question being "Why Jesus?" if we were in a court of law, the evidence presented up to this point would, without doubt, cause our attorney to argue that we have presented irrefutable proof that Jesus is the way, the truth, and the life. That no man can come to the Father but by him. Jesus is our King of kings and our Lord of lords.

We will continue now to present names and titles that apply to Jesus. If at any time you wish to ask Jesus to come into your life, ask Jesus to come into your life by saying this simple prayer: "I believe you are the son of God and you died on the cross for my sins. I ask you to come into my life and my heart and be my savior. Take my life and do something with it. In Jesus's name, I pray. Amen."

If you said that simple prayer, you are now a child of God and you belong to the family of God.

Congratulations, your life is about to get more exciting and wonderful than you have ever imagined.

God truly is a loving Father, and Jesus is a very loving savior.

We continue now with the names and titles that apply to Jesus:

- Faithful Witness

    And from Jesus Christ, who is the faithful witness, and the first begotten of the dead, and the prince of the kings of the earth. Unto him that loved us, and washed us from our sins in his own blood. (Revelation 1:5)

- First and Last

    And when I saw him, I fell at his feet as dead. And he laid his right hand upon me, saying unto me, "Fear not; I am the first and the last." (Revelation 1:17)

- First Begotten

    And from Jesus Christ, who is the faithful witness, and the first begotten of the dead, and the prince of the kings of the earth. Unto him that loved us, and washed us from our sins in his own blood. (Revelation 1:5)

- Forerunner

    Whither the forerunner is for us entered, even Jesus, made an high priest forever after the order of Mel-chis-e-dec. (Hebrews 6:20)

- Glory of the Lord

    And the glory of the Lord shall be revealed; and all flesh shall see it together; for the mouth of the Lord hath spoken it. (Isaiah 40:5)

- God

    The voice of him that crieth in the wilderness, Prepare ye the way of the Lord, make straight in the desert a highway for our God. (Isaiah 40:3)

- God Blessed

    Whose are the fathers, and of whom as concerning the flesh Christ came, who is over all, God blessed for ever; A-men. (Romans 9:5)

- Good Shepherd

    I am the good shepherd; the good shepherd giveth his life for the sheep. (John 10:11)

- Governor

    And thou Bethlehem; in the land of Juda, art not the least among the princes of Juda; for out of thee shall come a Governor, that shall rule thy people Israel. (Matthew 2:6)

- Great High Priest

    Seeing then that we have a great high priest, that is passed into the heavens, Jesus the son of God, let us hold fast our profession. Hebrews 4:14

- Head of the Church

    And hath put all things under his feet, and gave him to be the head over all things to the church. (Ephesians 1:22)

- Heir of All Things

    Hath in these last days spoken unto us by his Son, whom he hath appointed heir of all things, by whom also he made the worlds. (Hebrews 1:2)

- Holy Child

    For of a truth against thy holy child Jesus, whom thou hast anointed, both Herod, and Pontius Pilate, with the Gentiles, and the people of Israel, were gathered together. (Acts 4:27)

- Holy One

    But ye denied the Holy One and the Just, and desired a murderer to be granted unto you. (Acts 3:14)

- Holy One of God

    Saying, let us alone; what have we to do with thee; thou Jesus of Nazareth? Art thou come to destroy us? I know thee who thou art, the Holy One of God. (Mark 1:24)

- Holy One of Israel

    Fear not, thou worm Jacob, and ye men of Israel; I will help thee, saith the Lord, and thy redeemer, the Holy One of Israel. (Isaiah 41:14)

- Horn of Salvation

    And hath raised up an horn of salvation, for us in the house of his servant David. (Luke 1:69)

- I Am

    Jesus said unto them, "Verily, Verily, I say unto you, Before Abraham was, I am." (John 8:58)

- Image of God

    In whom the god of this world hath blinded the minds of them which believe not, lest the light of the glorious gospel of Christ, who is the image of God, should shine unto them. (2 Corinthians 4:4)

- Immanuel (God with us)

    Therefore; the Lord himself shall give you a sign, Behold, a virgin shall conceive, and bear a son, and shall call his name Immanuel. (Isaiah 7:14)

LOVE IS

- Jehovah's Anointed One

    The kings of the earth set themselves, and the rulers take counsel together, against the Lord, and against his anointed, saying. (Psalm 2:2)

- Jehovah (God Is Eternal)

    Trust ye in the Lord forever; for in the Lord Jehovah is everlasting strength. (Isaiah 26:4)

- Jesus (Savior of his People)

    And she shall bring forth a son, and thou shalt call his name JESUS, for he shall save his people from their sins. (Matthew 1:21)

- Jesus of Nazareth

    And the multitude said, This is Jesus, the prophet of Nazareth of Galilee. (Matthew 21:11)

- Judge of Israel

    Now gather thyself in troops, O daughter of troops; he hath laid siege against us: they shall smite the judge of Israel with a rod upon the cheek. (Micah 5:1)

- Just One

    Which of the prophets have not your fathers persecuted? And they have slain them which shewed before of the coming of the Just One, of whom you have been now the betrayers and murderers. (Acts 7:52)

- Jehovah Our Righteousness

    Behold, the days come, saith the Lord, that I will raise unto David a righteous Branch, and a King shall reign and prosper, and shall execute judgment and justice in the earth.
    In his days Judah shall be saved, and Israel shall dwell safely: and this is his name whereby he shall be called, THE LORD OUR RIGHTEOUSNESS. (Jeremiah 23:5–6)

- King

    Rejoice greatly, O daughter of Zion; shout, O daughter of Jerusalem; behold; thy King cometh unto thee; he is just, and having salvation; lowly, and riding upon an ass, and upon a colt the foal of an ass. (Zechariah 9:9)

- King Eternal

    Now unto the King eternal, immortal, invisible, the only wise God, be honour and glory for ever and ever. A-men. (1 Timothy 1:17)

- King of the Jews

    Saying, Where is he that is born King of the Jews? For we have seen his star in the east, and are come to worship him. (Matthew 2:2)

- King of Kings

    Which in his times he shall shew, who is the blessed and only Potentate, the King of kings, and Lord of lords. (1 Timothy 6:15)

LOVE IS

- Lawgiver

    For the Lord is our judge, the Lord is our lawgiver, the Lord is our King; he will save us. (Isaiah 33:22)

- Lamb

    And all that dwell upon the earth shall worship him, whose names are not written in the book of life of the Lamb slain from the foundation of the world. (Revelation 13:8)

- Lamb of God

    The next day John seeth Jesus coming unto him, and saith, Behold the Lamb of God, which taketh away the sin of the world. (John 1:29)

- Leader

    Behold, I have given him for a witness to the people, a leader and commander to the people. (Isaiah 55:4)

- Life

    Jesus saith unto him, "I am the way, the truth, and the life; no man cometh unto the Father, but by me." (John 14:6)

- Light

    The people that walked in darkness have seen a great light; they that dwell in the land of the shadow of death, upon them hath the light shined. (Isaiah 9:2)

I the Lord have called thee in righteousness, and will hold thine hand, and will keep thee for a covenant of the people, for a light of the Gentiles. (Isaiah 42:6)

The people which sat in darkness saw great light; and to them which sat in the region and shadow of death light is sprung up. (Matthew 4:16)

To give light to them that sit in darkness and in the shadow of death, to guide our feet into the way of peace. (Luke 1:79)

- Light

To him was life; and the life was the light of men.
And the light shineth in darkness; and the darkness comprehended it not.
There was a man sent from God, whose name was John.
The same came for a witness, to bear witness of that Light, that all men through him might believe.
He was not that Light, but was sent to bear witness of that Light.
That was the true Light, which lighteth every man that cometh into the world. (John 1:4–9)

Then spake Jesus again unto them saying, "I am the light of the world; he that followeth me shall not walk in darkness, but shall have the light of life." (John 8:12)

    Then Jesus said unto them, "Yet a little while is the light with you. Walk while ye have the light, lest darkness come upon you; for he that walketh in darkness knoweth not whither he goeth."
"While ye have light, believe in the light, that ye may be the children of light." These things spake Jesus, and departed, and did hide himself from them. John 12:35–36

    I am come a light unto the world, that whosoever believeth on me should not abide in darkness. (John 12:46)

    For God, who commanded the light to shine out of darkness, hath shined out of our hearts, to give the light of the knowledge of the glory of God in the face of Jesus Christ. (2 Corinthians 4:6)

    Wherefore he saith, Awake thou that sleepeth, and arise from the dead, and Christ shall give thee light. (Ephesians 5:14)

Let us discuss what we have read thus far. The question being, "Why Jesus? Why worship Jesus Christ?" Jesus being the Son of God; Jesus being the way, the truth, and the life; Jesus being the light of the world; and Jesus being the Savior who gave his blood for the sins of the world. We then have to include the fact that Jesus created the world and all that is in the world and without him was nothing made that was made. Jesus is the King of kings and the Lord of lords.

We all need to be loved. There is not one of us who would say they do not require love in their lives, for I have never met a man who was bold enough to say they could live alone and required no one.

When it comes to showing love, no one compares to Jesus. For who would know and understand what they were about to give because of love for mankind? In John 3:17 it is said, "For God sent not his Son into the world to condemn the world; but that the world through him might be saved." And in verse 18 it continues as follows, "He that believeth on him is not condemned; but he that believeth not is condemned already, because he hath not believed in the name of the only begotten Son of God."

Why Jesus? He gave everything for his creation. He held nothing back even to allowing himself to die on the cross for the world. Jesus said no man takes his life from him; he willingly gave his life.

> Jesus saith unto him, "I am the way, the truth, and the life, no man cometh unto the Father, but by me.
> If ye had known me, ye should have known my Father also: and from henceforth ye know him, and have seen him." (John 14:6–7)

> Let not your heart be troubled: ye believe in God, believe also in me.
> In my Fathers' house are many mansions: if it were not so, I would have told you: I go to prepare a place for you.
> And if I go and prepare a place for you, I will come again, and receive you unto myself; that where I am, there ye may be also.
> And whither I go ye know; and the way ye know. (John 14:1–4)

And the way you do know. He died on the cross that we might have everlasting life. All it takes from you is to believe that what I am saying is truth. Jesus said he is the way, the truth, and the life.

LOVE IS

If you believe what Jesus has said and you want to become a child of the living God, just say this simple prayer: "Dear Jesus, I believe you are the Son of God. I believe you died on the cross for me and rose again on the third day. I believe, Jesus, if I confess my sins, you are faithful and just to forgive my sins. So, Jesus, I ask you to come into my life, be my savior, and make something beautiful out of my life. Amen."

If you said that prayer, congratulations! You are now in the family of God. Jesus said he would never leave you or forsake you. Praise the Lord forever!

Let us now continue with the names and titles that apply to Jesus. As we do, let us meditate upon each of them. We realize the Old Testament speaks of Jesus as the New Testament does.

> Again a new commandment I write unto you, which thing is true in him and in you, because the darkness is past, and the true light now shineth.
>
> He that saith he is in the light, and hateth his brother, is in darkness even unto now.
>
> He that loveth his brother abideth in the light, and there is none occasion of stumbling in him. (1 John 2:8–10)

> And the city had no need of the sun, neither of the moon, to shine in it: for the glory of God did lighten it, and the Lamb is the light thereof. (Revelation 21:23)

> The Lord is my light and my salvation: whom shall I fear? The Lord is the strength of my life; of whom shall I be afraid? (Psalm 27:1)

> For with thee is the fountain of life: in thy light shall we see light. (Psalm 36:9)

God is the Lord, which hath shewed us light: bind the sacrifice with cords, even unto the horns of the alter. (Psalm 118:27)

Thy sun shall no more go down; neither shall thy moon withdraw itself; for the Lord shall be thine everlasting light, and the days of thy mourning shall be ended. (Isaiah 60:20)

Rejoice not against me, O mine enemy, when I fall, I shall arise. When I sit in darkness, the Lord shall be a light unto me. (Micah 7:8)

And his brightness was as the light, he had horns coming out of his hand; and there was the hiding of his power. (Habakkuk 3:4)

This then is the message which we have heard of him, and declare unto you, that God is light, and in him is no darkness at all. (1 John 1:5)

And there shall be no night there; and they need no candle, neither light of the sun; for the Lord God giveth them light: and they shall reign for ever and ever. (Revelation 22:5)

Thou shalt also decree a thing, and it shall be established unto thee, and the light shall shine upon thy ways. (Job 22:28)

Light is sown for the righteous, and gladness for the upright in heart. (Psalm 97:11)

Unto the upright there ariseth light in the darkness, he is gracious, and full of compassion, and righteous. (Psalm 112:4)

But the path of the just is as the shining light, that shineth more and more unto the perfect day. (Proverbs 4:18)

Then shall break forth as the morning, and thine health shall spring forth speedily; and thy righteousness shall go before thee; the glory of the Lord shall be thy rereward. (Isaiah 58:8)

The night is far spent the day is at hand; let us therefore cast off the works of darkness, and let us put on the armor of light. (Romans 13:12)

For ye were sometimes darkness, but now are ye light in the Lord; walk as children of light. (Ephesians 5:8)

That ye may be blameless and harmless, the sons of God, without rebuke in the midst of a crooked and perverse nation, among whom ye shine as lights in the world. (Philippians 2:15)

Ye are all the children of light, and the children of the day, we are not of the night, nor of darkness.
Therefore let us not sleep, as do others; but let us watch and be sober. (1 Thessalonians 5:5–6)

- The Lion of the Tribe of Juda

    And one of the elders saith unto me, Weep not, behold, the Lion of the tribe of Juda, the Root of David, hath prevailed to open the book, and to loose the seven seals thereof. (Revelation 5:5)

- Lord of All

    The word which God sent unto the children of Israel, preaching peace by Jesus Christ. (He is Lord of all.) (Acts 10:36)

- Lord of Glory

    Which none of the princes of this world knew: for had they known it, they would not have crucified the Lord of glory. (1 Corinthians 2:8)

- The Lord of Righteousness

    In his days Judah shall be saved, and Israel shall dwell safely, and this is his name whereby he shall be called, THE LORD OUR RIGHTEOUSNESS. (Jeremiah 23:6)

- Man of Sorrows

    He is despised and rejected of men; a man of sorrows, and acquainted with grief; and we hid as it were our faces from him; he was despised, and we esteemed him not. (Isaiah 53:3)

- Master

    And they came to him, and awoke him, saying, Master, master we perish. Then he arose, and rebuked the wind, and the raging of the water: and they ceased, and there was a calm. (Luke 8:24)

    And Jesus said, "Who touched me?" When all denied, Peter and they that were with him said, Master, the multitude throng thee and press thee, and sayest thou, "Who touched me?" (Luke 8:45)

    And it came to pass, as they departed from him, Peter said unto Jesus, Master, it is good for us to be here, and let us make three tabernacles; one for thee, and one for Moses, and one for E-li-as; not knowing what he said. (Luke 9:33)

    And John answered and said, Master, we saw one casting out devils in thy name; and we forbade him, because he followeth not with us. (Luke 9:49)

    And they lifted up their voices, and said, Jesus, Master, have mercy on us. (Luke 17:13)

- Messenger

    But last of all; he sent unto them his son, saying, They will reverence my son. (Matthew 21:37)

For I came down from heaven, not to do mine own will, but the will of him that sent me. (John 6:38)

But I know him; for I am from him, and he hath sent me. (John 7:29)

Jesus said unto them, "If God were your Father, ye would love me, for I proceeded forth and came from God, neither came I of myself, but he sent me." (John 8:42)

I must work the works of him that sent me, while it is day, the night cometh, when no man can work. (John 9:4)

Say ye of him, whom the Father hath sanctified, and sent into the world. Thou blasphemest: because I said, I am the Son of God. (John 10:36)

For I have given unto them the words which thou gavest me; and they have received them, and have known surely that I came out from thee, and they have believed that thou didst send me.
I pray for them; I pray not for the world, but for them which thou hast given me, for they are thine.
And all mine are thine, and thine are mine; and I am glorified in them.
And now I am no more in the world, but these are in the world, and I come to thee, Holy Father, keep through thine own name, those whom thou hast given me, that they may be one, as we are.
While I was with them in the world, I kept them in thy name; those that thou gavest me I

have kept, and none of them is lost, but the son of perdition; that the scripture might be fulfilled.

And now come I to thee; and these things I speak in the world, that they might have my joy fulfilled in themselves.

I have given them thy word: and the world hath hated them, because they are not of the world, even as I am not of the world.

I pray not that thou shouldest take them out of the world, but that thou shouldest keep them from the evil.

They are not of the world, even as I am not of the world.

Sanctify them through thy truth, thy word is truth.

As thou hast sent me into the world, even so have I also sent them into the world.

And for their sakes I sanctify myself, that they also might be sanctified through the truth.

Neither pray I for these alone, but for them also which shall believe on me through their word. That they all may be one as thou, Father, art in me, and I in thee, that they also may be one in us, that the world may believe that thou hast sent me. (John 17:8–21)

- Messenger of the Covenant

Behold, "I will send my messenger, and he shall prepare the way before me: and the Lord, whom ye seek, shall suddenly come to his temple, even the messenger of the covenant, whom ye delight in; behold, he shall come," saith the Lord of hosts. (Malachi 3:1)

Jesus is the messenger of the Father, the one and only begotten Son of God. He is the only one that could be trusted to convey the wishes of our God. Jesus is God. There is God the Father, the Son of God, and the Holy Spirit. The three in one, with the same intent, the same thoughts. We are ever on God's heart and mind. As 1 Corinthians 2:9–10 says, "But as it is written, Eye hath not seen, nor ear heard, neither have entered into the heart of man, the things which God hath prepared for them that love him. But God hath revealed them unto us by his Spirit: for the Spirit searcheth all things, yea, the deep things of God."

For we were made in the image of God. In Genesis, we find in chapter 1, verses 26–27, "And the Lord said, Let us make man in our image, a er our likeness; and let them have dominion over the fish of the sea, and over the fowl of the air, and over the cattle, and over all the earth, and over every creeping thing that creepeth upon the earth. So God created man in his own image, in the image of God created he him; male and female created he them."

God does not seem so far away when I began to relate to him by understanding that I was made in his image. This is not trying to bring God down to my level, but the opposite is true; it brings me to a higher level, closer to him. God has emotions and feelings just as we do. He does not seem so far away when I think on these things.

God is a righteous and holy God, and Jesus Christ was tempted as we are but without sin. Jesus can relate to our struggles because he was tempted.

Why Jesus?

- Messiah (Hebrew for Christ, Anointed)

    And Simon Peter answered and said, Thou art the Christ, the Son of the living God. (Matthew 16:16)

    For unto you is born this day in the city of David; a Savior, which is Christ the Lord. (Luke 2:11)

And when eight days were accomplished for the circumcising of the child, his name was called JESUS, which was so named of the angel before he was conceived in the womb. (Luke 2:21)

And the devils came out of many, crying out, and saying Thou art Christ the Son of God, And he rebuking them suffered them not to speak; for they knew that he was Christ. (Luke 4:41)

"Ought not Christ to have suffered these things, and to enter into his glory?" (Luke 24:26)

He first findeth his own brother Simon, and saith unto him, We have found the Messiah, which is being interpreted, the Christ. (John 1:41)

Jesus saith unto her, "I that speak unto thee am he." (John 4:26)

And we believe and are sure that thou art that Christ, the Son of the living God. (John 6:69)

Others said, This is the Christ. But some said, Shall Christ come out of Galilee? (John 7:41)

She saith unto him, Yea, Lord: I believe that thou art the Christ, the Son of God, which should come into the world. (John 11:27)

But Saul increased the more in strength, and confounded the Jews: which dwelt at Damascus, proving that this is very Christ. (Acts 9:22)

Opening and alleging, that Christ must needs have suffered, and risen again from the dead, and that this Jesus, whom I preach unto you, is Christ. (Acts 17:3)

Whomsoever believeth that Jesus is the Christ is born of God: and everyone that loveth him that begat: loveth him also that is begotten of him. (1 John 5:1)

- Mighty God

For unto us a child is born, unto us a son is given; and the government shall be upon his shoulder; and his name shall be called Wonderful, Counsellor, The Mighty God, The Everlasting Father, The Prince of Peace. (Isaiah 9:6)

- Morning Star

"I Jesus have sent mine angel to testify unto you these things in the churches, I am the root and the offspring of David, and the bright and morning star." (Revelation 22:16)

- Our Passover

Purge out therefore the old leaven, that ye may be a new lump, as ye are unleavened. For even Christ our Passover is sacrificed for us.
(1 Corinthians 5:7)

- Perfect Man

And he made his grave with the wicked, and with the rich in his death; because he had done no violence, neither was any deceit in his mouth. (Isaiah 53:9)

And the word was made flesh, and dwelt among us, (and we beheld his glory, the glory as of the only begotten of the Father), full of grace and truth. (John 1:14)

For he hath made him to be sin for us, who knew no sin, that we might be made the righteousness of God in him. (2 Corinthians 5:21)

And being made perfect, he became the author of eternal salvation unto all them that obey him. (Hebrews 5:9)

- Prince of Kings

    And from Jesus Christ, who is the faithful witness, and the first begotten of the dead, and the prince of the kings of the earth. Unto him that loved us, and washed us from our sins in his own blood. (Revelation 1:5)

- Prince of Life

    And killed the Prince of life, whom God hath raised from the dead, whereof we are witnesses. (Acts 3:15)

- Prince of Peace

    For unto us a child is born, unto us a son is given; and the government shall be upon his shoulder, and his name shall be called Wonderful,

Counsellor, The Mighty God, The everlasting Father, The Prince of Peace. (Isaiah 9:6)

- Prophet

    I will raise them up a Prophet from among their brethren, like unto thee, and will put my words in his mouth, and he shall speak unto them all that I shall command him. (Deuteronomy 18:18)

    And the multitude said, This is Jesus, the prophet of Nazareth of Galilee. (Matthew 21:11)

    But when they sought to lay hands on him, they feared the multitude, because they took him for a prophet. (Matthew 21:46)

    And there came a fear on all: and they glorified God, saying, That a great prophet is risen up among us; and That God hath visited his people. (Luke 7:16)

    Nevertheless I must walk today, and tomorrow, and the day following: for it cannot be that a prophet perish out of Jerusalem. (Luke 13:33)

    And he said unto them, "What things?" And they said unto him, Concerning Jesus of Nazareth, which was a prophet mighty in deed and word before God and all the people. (Luke 24:19)

    The woman saith unto him, Sir, I perceive that thou art a prophet. (John 4:19)

Then those men, when they had seen the miracle that Jesus did, said, This is of a truth that prophet that should come into the world. (John 6:14)

Many of the people therefore, when they heard this saying, said, Of the truth this is the Prophet. (John 7:40)

They say unto the blind man again, What sayest thou of him, that he hath opened thine eyes? He said, He is a prophet. (John 9:17)

For Moses truly said unto the fathers, A Prophet shall the Lord your God raise up unto you of your brethren, like unto me: him shall ye hear in all things whatsoever he shall say unto you. (Acts 3:22)

- Redeemer

For I know that my redeemer liveth, and that he shall stand at the latter day upon the earth. (Job 19:25)

- Resurrection and Life

Jesus said unto her, "I am the resurrection, and the life: he that believeth in me, though he were dead, yet shall he live." (John 11:25)

- Rock

And he shall be for a sanctuary, but for a stone of stumbling and for a rock of offence to both the houses of Israel, for a gin and for a snare to the inhabitants of Jerusalem. (Isaiah 8:14)

Wherefore? Because they sought it not by faith, but as it were by the works of the law, For they stumbled at that stumbling stone. (Romans 9:32)

And a stone of stumbling, and a rock of offence, even to them which stumble at the word, being disobedient; whereunto also they were appointed. (1 Peter 2:8)

And did all drink the same spiritual drink, for they drank of that spiritual Rock, that followed them, and that Rock was Christ. (1 Corinthians 10:4)

- Root of David

    "I Jesus have sent mine angel to testify unto you these things in the churches, I am the root and the offspring of David, and the bright and morning star." (Revelation 22:16)

- Rose of Sharon

    I am the rose of Sharon and the lily of the valleys. (Song of Solomon 2:1)

- Savior

    For unto you is born this day in the city of David a Savior, which is Christ the Lord. (Luke 2:11)

- Seed of Woman

    And I will put enmity between thee and the woman, and between thy seed and her seed; it shall bruise thy head, and thou shalt bruise his heel. (Genesis 3:15)

    But when the fullness of the time was come, God sent forth his Son, made of a woman, made under the law. (Galatians 4:4)

- Shiloh

    The scepter shall not depart from Judah, nor a lawgiver from between his feet, until Shiloh come, and unto him shall the gathering of the people be. (Genesis 49:10)

- Son of the Blessed

    But he held his peace, and answered nothing. Again that high priest asked him, and said unto him, Art thou the Christ, the Son of the Blessed. (Mark 14:61)

- Son of David

    The book of the generation of Jesus Christ, the son of David, the son of Abraham. (Matthew 1:1)

- Son of God

    And was there until the death of Herod, that it might be fulfilled which was spoken of the

Lord by the prophet, saying, out of Egypt have I called my son. (Matthew 2:15)

- Son of the Highest

    He shall be great, and shall be called the Son of the Highest, and the Lord God shall give unto him the throne of his father David. (Luke 1:32)

- Son of Man

    And Jesus saith unto him, "The foxes have holes, and the birds of the air have nests; but the Son of man hath not where to lay his head." (Matthew 8:20)

- Sun of Righteousness

    But unto you that fear my name shall the Sun of Righteousness arise with healing in his wings, and ye shall go forth, and grow up as calves of the stall. (Malachi 4:2)

- Star of Jacob

    I shall see him, but not now, I shall behold him, but not neigh; there shall come a Star out of Jacob, and a Scepter shall rise out of Israel, and shall smite the comers of Moab and destroy all the children of Sheth. (Numbers 24:17)

- Sun

    Their line is gone out through all the earth, and their words to the end of the world. In them hath he set a tabernacle for the sun. (Psalm 19:4)

LOVE IS

- Servant of the Lord

   He shall see of the travail of his soul, and shall be satisfied by his knowledge shall my righteous servant justify many: for he shall bear their iniquities. (Isaiah 53:11)

- True Light

   That was the true Light, which lighteth every man that cometh into the world. (John 1:9)

- True Vine

   I am the true vine and my Father is the husbandman.
   Every branch in me that beareth not fruit he taketh away, and every branch that beareth fruit, he purgeth it, that it may bring forth more fruit.
   Now we are clean through the word which I have spoken unto you.
   Abide in me and I in you. As the branch cannot bear fruit of itself, except it abide in the vine, no more can ye, except ye abide in me.
   I am the vine, ye are the branches: He that abideth in me, and I in him, the same bringeth forth much fruit, for without me ye can do nothing.
   If a man abide not in me, he is cast forth as a branch, and is withered; and men gather them, and cast them into the fire, and they are burned.
   If ye abide in me, and my words abide in you, ye shall ask what ye will, and it shall be done unto you.
   Herein is my Father glorified that ye bear much fruit, so shall ye be my disciples.

> As the Father hath loved me, so have I loved you, continue ye in my love.
>
> If ye keep my commandments, ye shall abide in my love, even as I have kept my Father's commandments, and abide in his love.
>
> These things have I spoken unto you, that my joy might remain in you, and that your joy might be full.
>
> This is my commandment, That ye love one another, as I have loved you.
>
> Greater love hath no man than this, that a man lay down his life for his friends. (John 15:1–13)

This is it! This is why Jesus. For he did lay down his life for you and me. In John 3:16, we read, "For God so loved the world that he gave his only begotten Son, that whosoever believeth in him should not perish, but have everlasting life."

What a savior! All you have to do is say a simple prayer, then turn your life over to Jesus. He will never leave you or forsake you. The Bible says the angels in heaven celebrate when one sinner turns his life over to Jesus.

If you want to get saved, say this simple prayer: "Dear Jesus, I believe you gave your life that I might live. I ask you to forgive my sins. Prepare me to live an eternity with you and make my life pleasing to you. I believe I am now in the family of God, and you, Jesus, are my savior forever. Amen!"

> Ye are my friends if you do whatsoever I command you.
>
> Henceforth I call you not servants, for the servant knoweth not what his lord doeth: but I have called you friends; for all things that I have heard of my Father, I have made known unto you.

LOVE IS

You have not chosen me, but I have chosen you, and ordained you, that ye should go and bring forth fruit, and that your fruit should remain, that whatsoever you should ask of the Father in my name, he may give it you.

These things I command you, that ye love one another.

If the world hate you, ye know that it hated me before it hated you.

If ye were of the world, the world would love his own; but because you are not of the world, but I have chosen you out of the world, therefore the world hateth you.

Remember the word that I said unto you. The servant is not greater than his lord, If they have persecuted me, they will also persecute you: if they have kept my saying they will keep yours also.

But all these things will they do unto you for my name's sake, because they know not him that sent me.

If I had not come and spoken unto them, they had not had sin, but now they have no cloke for their sin.

He that hateth me hateth my Father also.

If I had not done among them the works which none other man did, they had not had sin, but now have they both seen and hated both me and my Father.

But this cometh to pass, that the word might be fulfilled that is written in their law. They hated me without a cause.

But when the Comforter is come, whom I will send unto you from the Father, even the Spirit of truth, which proceedeth from the Father, he shall testify of me.

And ye also shall bear witness, because ye have been with me from the beginning. (John 15:14–27)

- Word

In the beginning was the Word, and the Word was with God, and the Word was God.

The same was in the beginning with God.

All things were made by him; and without him was not anything made that was made. In him was life; and the life was the light of men. (John 1:1–4)

- Water of Life

Then saith the woman of Samaria unto him, How is it that thou, being a Jew, asketh drink of me, which am a woman of Samaria? For the Jews have no dealings with the Samaritans.

Jesus answered and said unto her, "If thou knewest the gift of God, and who it is that saith to thee, Give me to drink; thou wouldest have asked of him, and he would have given thee living water."

The woman saith unto him "Sir, thou hast nothing to draw with, and the well is deep; from whence then hast thou that living water?"

"Art thou greater than our Father Jacob, which gave us the well, and drank thereof himself, and his children and his cattle?"

Jesus answered and said unto her, "Whosoever drinketh of this water shall thirst again."

"But whosoever drinketh of the water that I shall give him shall never thirst: but the water that I shall give him shall be in him a well of water springing up into everlasting life." (John 4:9–14)

This completes the names and titles given to Jesus in the Word of God. When we read them and note the expansiveness of Jesus and what he has done and what he is willing to do for each of us, how can we not worship our King? How can we not praise him for the love he possesses?

Jesus laid down his life that we might live. He took our punishment. He died and went to hell for us so we would not have to. He paid the ransom. He could have walked away, but he chose to pay the price. Why Jesus? This is why!

The third part of the Godhead as mentioned earlier is the Holy Spirit of God. Nothing can be accomplished without the aid of the Holy Spirit. The Holy Spirit being the one who speaks to you, who calls you out of the world into salvation and peace. The Holy Spirit being our teacher, our comforter, the one who draws us to Christ in the day of salvation. He is ever with us, never to leave us alone. It is written in 1 Corinthians 12:7–11:

> But the manifestation of the Spirit is given to every man to profit withal.
> For to one is given by the Spirit the word of wisdom, to another the word of knowledge by the same Spirit.
> To another faith by the same Spirit, to another the gifts of healing by the same Spirit; to another the working of miracles; to another prophecy; to another discerning of spirits; to another divers kinds of tongues; to another the interpretation of tongues;
> But all these worketh that one and selfsame Spirit, dividing to every man severely as he will.

But now hath God set the members every one of them in the body, as it hath pleased him. (1 Corinthians 12:18)

And when Paul had laid his hands upon them, the Holy Ghost came upon them, and they spake with tongues, and prophesied. (Acts 19:6)

And these signs shall follow them that believe; In my name shall they cast out devils; they shall speak with new tongues. (Mark 16:17)

Jesus answered and said unto him, Verily, verily, I say unto thee, Except a man be born again, he cannot see the kingdom of God. (John 3:3)

Jesus answered, Verily, verily, I say unto thee, Except a man be born of water and of the Spirit, he cannot enter into the kingdom of God.
That which is born of the flesh is flesh; and that which is born of the Spirit is spirit. (John 3:5–6)

Then remembered I the word of the Lord, how that he said, John indeed baptized with water; but ye shall be baptized with the Holy Ghost. (Acts 11:16)

And the Spirit of the Lord shall rest upon him, the spirit of wisdom and understanding, the spirit of counsel and might, the spirit of knowledge and of the fear of the Lord. (Isaiah 11:2)

For I will pour water upon him that is thirsty, and floods upon the dry ground: I will pour my spirit upon thy seed, my blessing upon thine offspring. (Isaiah 44:3)

The Spirit of the Lord God is upon me: because the Lord hath anointed me to preach good tidings unto the meek: he hath sent me to bind up the brokenhearted, to proclaim liberty to the captives, and the opening of the prison to them that are bound. (Isaiah 61:1)

God is a Spirit and they that worship him worship him in spirit and in truth. (John 4:24)

For the law of the Spirit of life in Christ Jesus hath made me free from the law of sin and death. (Romans 8:2)

The Spirit itself beareth witness with our spirit, that we are the children of God. (Romans 8:16)

Likewise the Spirit also helpeth our infirmities: for we know not what we should pray for as we ought: but the Spirit itself maketh intercession for us with groanings which cannot be uttered. (Romans 8:26)

Now the Lord is that Spirit: and where the Spirit of the Lord is there is liberty. (2 Corinthians 3:17)

But the fruit of the Spirit is love, joy, peace, longsuffering, gentleness, goodness, faith. (Galatians 5:22)

And grieve not the holy Spirit of God, whereby ye are sealed unto the day of redemption. (Ephesians 4:30)

Quench not the Spirit. (1 Thessalonians 5:19)

For the Word of God is quick and powerful, and sharper than any two edged sword, piercing even to the dividing asunder of soul and spirit, and of the joints and marrow, and is a discerner of thoughts and intents of the heart. (Hebrews 4:12)

But let it be the hidden man of the heart, in that which is not corruptible, even the ornament of a meek and quiet spirit, which is in the sight of God of great price. (1 Peter 3:4)

And the Spirit and the bride say, Come. And let him that is athirst come, And whosoever will, let him take the water of life freely. (Revelation 22:17)

John answered, saying unto them all, I indeed baptize you with water, but one mightier than I cometh, the latchet of whose shoes I am not worthy to unloose: he shall baptize you with the Holy Ghost and with fire. (Luke 3:16)

But as it is written, Eye hath not seen, nor ear heard, neither have entered into the heart of man, the things which God hath prepared for them that love him. (1 Corinthians 2:9)

> But God hath revealed them unto us by his Spirit; for the Spirit searcheth all things, yea, the deep things of God. (1 Corinthians 2:10)
>
> For what man knoweth the things of a man, save the spirit of man which is in him? Even so the things of God knoweth no man, but the Spirit of God. (1 Corinthians 2:11)
>
> Now we have received not the spirit of the world, but the spirit which is of God; that we might know the things that are freely given to us of God. (1 Corinthians 2:12)
>
> But of him are ye in Christ Jesus, who of God is made unto us wisdom, and righteousness; and sanctification, and redemption.
> That, according as it is written, He that glorieth, let him glory in the Lord. (1 Corinthians 1:30–31)

The best way to relate the truth about God is to quote the Bible. When relating events in our lives, there will always be those who do not believe their ears. People tend to release stories they hear due to their desire to prove these spiritual events to be not true. By receiving events into our belief system, we must then accept them as truth. If we accept as truth a spiritual event, we commit ourselves to a way of life that demands of us a commitment to truth. This would in turn demand a commitment to living a life of a higher level of consciousness. It may not always be easy to turn ourselves in the right direction and remain face on, but it is worth it. Oh, how it is worth it.

God has many wonderful gifts awaiting each of us. When walking down that path to God is the only path we will allow ourselves to walk, we then begin to experience awesome events that bring more happiness than we ever thought possible.

This is God! You know that you have stepped into the kingdom for which you were created. The kingdom of God whose king is Jesus Christ and his Father, Father God. Then there is the Holy Spirit who does not speak of himself but of Jesus. Jesus speaks of his Father; our Father God speaks of the Trinity of God. There is faith, there is hope, and there is love. There greatest of these is love. What each of us long for is freely given in the kingdom of God.

> And the Lord spake unto Moses, saying,
> Speak unto Aaron and unto his sons, saying, On this wise ye shall bless the children of Israel, saying unto them,
> The Lord bless thee, and keep thee,
> The Lord make his face shine upon thee, and be gracious unto thee:
> The Lord lift up his countenance upon thee, and give thee peace.
> And they shall put my name upon the children of Israel: and I will bless them. (Numbers 6:22–27)

> For as many as are led by the Spirit of God; they are the sons of God.
> For ye have not received the spirit of bondage again to fear; but he have received the Spirit of adoption, whereby we cry Ab'-ba Father.
> The Spirit itself beareth witness with our spirit, that we are the children of God.
> And if children, then heirs; heirs of God, and joint heirs with Christ: if so be that we suffer with him, that we may be also glorified together.
> For I reckon that the sufferings of this present time are not worthy to be compared with the glory which shall be revealed in us. (Romans 8:14–18)

The words of a talebearer are as wounds, and they go down into the innermost parts of the bearer. (Proverbs 26:22)

- *Our words create our world.*

Where no wood is, there the fire goeth out: so where there is no talebearer, the strife ceaseth. (Proverbs 26:20)

A word fitly spoken is like apples of gold in pictures of silver. (Proverbs 25:11)

But I say unto you. That every idle word that man shall speak, they shall give account thereof in the day of judgment. (Matthew 12:36)

For by thou words, thou shalt be justified, and by thou words thou shalt be condemned. (Matthew 12:37)

Heavens and earth shall pass away, but my words shall not pass away. (Matthew 24:35)

Then Simon Peter answered him, Lord, to whom shall we go? Thou hast the words of eternal life. (John 6:68)

Let the word of Christ dwell in you richly in all wisdom, teaching and admonishing one another in psalms and hymns and spiritual songs, singing with grace in your hearts to the Lord. (Colossians 3:16)

For our gospel came not unto you in word only, but also in power, and in the Holy Ghost, and in much assurance; as ye know what manner of men we were among you for your sake. (1 Thessalonians 1:5)

Wherefore comfort one another with these words. (1 Thessalonians 4:18)

Study to shew thyself approved unto God, a workman that needeth not to be ashamed, rightly dividing the word of truth. (2 Timothy 2:15)

Preach the word; be instant in season, out of season, reprove, rebuke, exhort with all long suffering and doctrine. (2 Timothy 4:2)

For the word of God is quick and powerful and sharper than any two edged sword, piercing even to the dividing asunder of soul and spirit, and of the joints and marrow, and is a discerner of the thoughts and intents of the heart. (Hebrew 4:12)

But be ye doers of the word, and not hearers only, deceiving your own selves. (James 1:22)

Being born again, not of corruptible seed, but of incorruptible, by the word of God, which liveth and abideth forever. (1 Peter 1:23)

As newborn babes, desire the sincere milk of the word, that ye may grow thereby. (1 Peter 2:2)

Likewise, ye wives, be in subjection to your own husbands, that, if any obey not the word, they also may without the word be won by the conversation of the wives. (1 Peter 3:1)

That which was from the beginning, which we have heard, which we have seen with our eyes, which we have looked upon, and our hands have handled, of the Word of life. (1 John 1:1)

But whoso keepeth his word, in him verily is the love of God perfected; hereby know we that we are in him. (1 John 2:5)

My little children, let us not love in word, neither in tongue; but in deed and in truth. (1 John 3:18)

And if any man shall take away from the words of the book of this prophecy, God shall take away his part out of the book of life, and out of the holy city, and from the things which are written in this book. (Revelation 22:19)

Death and life are in the power of the tongue; and they that love it shall eat the fruit thereof. (Proverbs 18:21)

The Lord bless thee and keep thee. The Lord make his face shine upon thee and be gracious unto thee. The Lord lift up his countenance upon thee and give thee peace. And they shall put my name upon the children of Israel, and I will bless them. (Numbers 6:24–27)

Grace Wins Every Time

God has provided everything we need to live an overcoming life. There are times in life when it seems life has become a continuing fight. As we become entrenched in the struggle and sometimes feel that we have begun to lose the battle, the Holy Spirit will always come to our rescue. He lets us know there is no reason to fight. He will do our fighting for us. *Exodus 14:14* tells us, *"The Lord shall fight for you, and ye shall hold your peace."* The Holy Spirit will help with every problem. He is present to comfort us, to guide us, to speak to us, and to fight our battles for us. The Bible says he is a very present help in the time of trouble.

There is something to be said for the struggle we must become friendly with. There is no learning by being held in some odd, painless place. We must face opposition to gain strength. God knows this. He provides the door to the other side of this power struggle that we are sure to encounter. There will be, without a doubt, many struggles the enemy will throw at us. The enemy stands no chance against a child of God. God's greatest pleasure is providing help for his children. He never has and never will fail.

The strength you feel would never have become your friend had you not been through life's struggles. God knew this. He now looks at us with pride on his face for the fight you now have been through. He knows we cannot be handed our dreams without some form of personal affront having knocked us down a time or two. As was stated before, God says he will fight our battles for us. This is the intent of our Father for the children he loves so much. At the same time, he does not want a coward to quiver at the sight of his enemies. He wants us to stand up to our enemy in assurance of his capability to make right the attack from our enemy. The strength we need to rely upon comes from God our Father. God enjoys proving his strength to his children. His love for us is a consuming fire that will never go out.

There are, in our future, assignments that have to be fulfilled. We are not to be idle here on earth or in heaven. Idleness is an enemy. Your creativeness disappears with idleness.

With God comes miracles, signs, and wonders. This is what we see when we have a relationship with Christ. Why would we believe it would be different in eternity? It will not be different. We have an amazing future to look forward to. If indeed we see signs and wonders here on earth, how much more shall we see when we step into heaven?

Heaven is the ultimate goal. This is why people try so hard to tell others about Jesus Christ and our Father God. We are not trying to push our savior on anyone. When we see others whom we know are lost, it hurts our hearts to know their destination is not heaven but indeed hell. People mistake caring for preaching. What kind of people would we be if indeed we told no one about Jesus? Telling others is an act of love. No greater love has no man but that he lay down his life for his friends. Jesus has shown this kind of *love*.

On the cross at Calvary, Jesus laid down his life to make it possible for you and me to not go to hell but instead go to heaven. There we will spend an eternity with Jesus Christ. No one took his life; he gave his life for you and me. Have you ever known such great love as Jesus gives?

How wonderful Jesus is! If you want to accept Jesus as your savior, just say a simple prayer asking Jesus to come into your heart and life right now. If you would like to do this, repeat this simple prayer after me: *"Dear Jesus, I believe you are the Son of God. I believe you died on the cross and rose on the third day. Please come into my life and do something with it. Do with me what you need to do. In Jesus's name! Amen!"*

The book of facts that completes the information in this book is a very convenient form of how-to and where-to to have at your fingertips. The concordance in the back of your Bible is a very convenient addition to any Bible but is lacking in helpful information, whereas the one I have included is a thorough informational asset.

To explain what you will find, the first part will compare what you will find first in the Old Testament and then in the New Testament, ergo, OT = Old Testament and NT = New Testament. This is a valuable addition when showing the relevance between the Old Testament and the New Testament.

The information in this part of the book is put here to be of assistance to the reader for his benefit only.

The third part of the Godhead as mentioned earlier is the Holy Spirit of God, by which nothing can be accomplished without his aid. The Holy Spirit being the one who speaks to you, who calls you out of the world into his salvation and peace. The Holy Spirit being our teacher, our comforter, the one that draws us to Christ in the day of salvation. He is ever with us, never to leave us alone. It is written in 1 Corinthians 12:7–11, "But the manifestation of the Spirit is given to every man to profit withal. For to one is given by the Spirit the word of wisdom, to another the word of knowledge by the same Spirit. To another faith by the same Spirit; to another the gifts of healing by the same Spirit. To another the working of miracles; to another prophecy; to another discerning of spirits; to another divers kinds of tongues; to another interpretation of tongues; But all these worketh that one and the same Spirit, dividing to every man severally as he will," and in 1 Corinthians 12:18, "But now hath God set the members every one of them in the Body, as it hath pleased Him."

God has chosen us to be in his body of believers. He wishes that no one be left out. *John 3:16 tells us that God so loved the world that he gave his only begotten Son that whosoever believeth should not perish but have everlasting life.*

When Christ was crucified, he said, *"No one takes his life, but he gave his life of his own free will for you and me."* What a love that has been bestowed upon us!

LOVE IS

To show the relevance between the Old Testament and the New Testament, the following section is presented to you for this purpose.

In each example, you will find an OT, which represents the Old Testament. Immediately following you will find an NT, which represents the New Testament.

Book of Facts

> For had ye believed Moses, Ye would have believed me: for be wrote of me. But if ye believe not his writings, how shall ye believe my words? (John 5:46–47)

Jesus and his true church is the light.

OT Jesus is the light
Genesis 1:3
Micah 7:8
Isaiah 60:1–2, 20
Isaiah 49:6
Isaiah 30:26
Isaiah 9:2
Isaiah 5:20
Proverbs 4:18
Psalm 119:130, 105
Psalm 97:2
Psalm 36:9
Psalm 27:1
Psalm 4:6
2 Samuel 23:4
Isaiah 42:6
Psalm 84:2
Psalm 118:27
Habakkuk 3:4
Job 22:28
Psalm 112:4

Isaiah 58:8
2 Chronicles 5:13–14

NT Jesus is the light
1 John 1:5–7
Ephesians 5:8–14
2 Corinthians 4:4–6
Acts 26:18
John 1:1–10
John 3:19
John 8:12
John 12:35–36
Matthew 5:14–16
Matthew 4:16
1 Corinthians 4:5
Acts 13:47
John 1:4, 9
Revelation 21:23
Luke 1:79
1 John 2:8, 10
Revelation 22:5
John 9:4
Romans 13:12
Philippians 2:15
1 Thessalonians 5:5–6
John 12:44–46

Jesus would be seed of the woman.
OT Genesis 3:15
NT Galatians 4:4

Jesus would come through seed of Abraham.
OT Genesis 12:3
NT Matthew 1:1

Jesus would come
through seed of Isaac.
OT Genesis 17:19
NT Luke 3:34

Jesus would come through
tribe of Judah.
OT Genesis 49:10
NT Luke 3:33

Jesus is anointed and eternal.

OT Psalm 45:6–7
Psalm 102:25–27
NT Hebrews 1:8–12
Mark 14:1–9

Jesus was born of a virgin.
OT Genesis 3:15
Isaiah 7:14

NT Luke 2:4–7

Jesus's flight into Egypt.
OT Hosea 11:1
NT Matthew 2:14–15

God declared Jesus
to be his Son.
OT Psalm 2:7
NT Matthew 3:17

Jesus would come
through seed of Jacob.
OT Numbers 24:17
NT Matthew 1:2

Jesus is heir to the
throne of David.
OT Isaiah 9:7
NT Luke 1:32–33

Jesus would be born
in Bethlehem.
OT Micah 5:2
NT Luke 2:4–7

Children slaughtered
at Jesus's birth.
OT Jeremiah 31:15
NT Matthew 2:16–18

Jesus was preceded
by a forerunner.
OT Malachi 3:1
NT Luke 7:24–27

Jesus's Galilean ministry.
OT Isaiah 9:1–2
NT Matthew 4:13–16

LOVE IS

Jesus would teach
using parables.
OT Psalm 78:2–4
NT Matthew 13:34–35

Jesus was rejected
by his people.
OT Isaiah 53:3
NT John 1:11
Luke 23:18

Jesus sent to heal
brokenhearted
OT Isaiah 61:1–2
NT Luke 4:18–19

Jesus was not believed.

OT Isaiah 53:1
NT John 12:37–38

Jesus's entry into
Jerusalem as King.
OT Zechariah 9:9
NT Mark 11:7–11

Jesus was adored by infants.

OT Psalm 8:2
NT Matthew 21:15–16

Jesus is priest in the
order of Melchizedek.
OT Psalm 104:4
NT Hebrews 5:5–6

Jesus was betrayed for
tiny pieces of silver.
OT Zechariah 11:12
NT Matthew 26:14–15

Jesus was betrayed by a friend.

OT Psalm 41:9
NT Luke 22:47–48

Jesus was silent to accusation.

OT Isaiah 53:7
NT Mark 15:4–5

Jesus was accused by
false witnesses.
OT Psalm 35:11
NT Mark 14:57–58

Jesus was hated without a cause.
OT Psalm 35:19
NT John 15:24–25

Jesus was pierced through his hands and feet.
OT Zechariah 12:10
NT John 20:27

Jesus was reproached by the people.
OT Psalm 69:9
NT Romans 15:3

Jesus's side was pierced.

OT Zechariah 12:10
NT John 19:32–36

Jesus was resurrected.
OT Psalm 16:10
NT Mark 16:6–7

Old Testament was written for future generations.
NT 1 Corinthians 10:11

Jesus was spat upon and beaten.
OT Isaiah 50:6
NT Matthew 26:67

Jesus was sacrificed for us.

OT Isaiah 53:5
NT Romans 5:6–8

Jesus's side was pierced.

OT Zechariah 12:10
NT John 19:32–36

Jesus was put to death without broken bones.
OT Psalm 34:20
NT John 19:32–36

Jesus was buried with the rich.
OT Isaiah 53:9
NT Matthew 27:57–60

Jesus ascended to our Father's right hand.
OT Psalm 68:18
NT Mark 16:19
1 Corinthians 15:4
Ephesians 4:8

Jesus is complete Word of God.
NT Hebrews 10:7
John 1:1–5
Revelation 19:11–13
11 Corinthians 4:6

Jesus foretold of all things.
Mark 13:23

Jesus quoted Psalm 110:1 to show the Pharisees that Jesus was both son of David and Son of God.
Luke 20:42

Jesus taught that we have the words of Moses (the Law) and the prophets to teach us about Jesus.
Luke 16:29–31

Jesus said all things must be fulfilled which were written in the law of Moses, by the prophets, and in Psalms concerning Jesus.
Luke 24:44

Jesus told the Jews that sought to kill him that they did not know our Father. Jesus told them to search the scriptures, for they testify of Jesus.
John 5:17–39

Jesus taught that all of God's Word is our true food.
Matthew 4:4

Notice Jesus said "every word."
God used the Old Testament to promise to send his son, Jesus Christ.
Romans 1:1–3

God used the Old Testament to teach, the just shall live by faith.
Romans 1:17, Habakkuk 2:4

God used the Old Testament to show how the Jews blasphemed God's name among the Gentiles.

Romans 2:17–24
Isaiah 52:5
Ezekiel 36:22

God used the Old Testament to teach that he would not forsake his people for his name's sake.

1 Samuel 12:22

God did not destroy Israel for his name's sake.

Ezekiel 20:7–10
Ezekiel 20:19–22
Numbers 14:11–24

God commanded to teach his word to our children.

Deuteronomy 6:4–12

Paul taught part of the armor of God is the sword of the Spirit, which is the Word of God.

Ephesians 6:10–17

The story of Abraham's faith being counted to him as righteousness.

Genesis 15:1–6 was not written just for his sake but was written for us also, to whom our faith shall be counted as righteousness if we believe on him that raised up Jesus, our Lord, from the dead.

Romans 4:1–25

Now all these things happened unto them for examples, and they are written for our admonition, upon whom the ends of the world are come.
1 Corinthians 10:11

Paul taught to study the complete Word of God.
2 Timothy 2:15

Paul taught to read God's Word in church.
Colossians 4:16

The Song of Moses and the Song of the Lamb
Deuteronomy 31:22, Deuteronomy 32:44, Revelation 15:1–3

Jesus fulfilled the prophets.
Matthew 2:15

Jesus taught us to search for double references in prophecy.
Luke 4:14–21
Isaiah 61:1–5

By reading the Scripture in church, Jesus was teaching to interpret Scripture literally.

Jesus was prophesied to come, first coming as King, and double prophecy showed his Second Coming as King.
Matthew 21:4–5, Zechariah 9:9–10

Jesus said to read Daniel to see the event of the end.
Matthew 24:15
Daniel 9:26–27

Jesus said to read Genesis (days of Noah) to see Second Coming.
Matthew 24:37
Genesis chapter six

The thing that has been, it is that which shall be.
Ecclesiastes 1:9

God's Word

Purpose for God's Word
2 Timothy 3:15-17
- Brings faith

Romans 10:17
- Makes man wise to salvation

2 Timothy 3:15
Psalm 19:7–11
Psalm 119:50
Ezekiel 37:1–28
Matthew 16:13–20
Luke 16:16
Romans 1:16
Romans 10:1–17
- Is man's protection

Ephesians 6:10–20
- Protects from lies

Matthew 4:1–11
Matthew 22:23–33
2 Corinthians 2:14–17
2 Corinthians 4:1–6
2 Peter 3:16
- Is our sword for battle

Isaiah 11:4
Ephesians 6:17
2 Thessalonians 2:8
Hebrews 4:12
Revelation 1:16
Revelation 2:12
Revelation 2:16
- Is our armor

Ephesians 6:10–19
Psalm 91:4
Romans 13:12
2 Corinthians 6:7
1 Thessalonians 5:8
- Is a flame to consume our enemy

Jeremiah 5:14
Jeremiah 23:29
Exodus 4:20
2 Kings 6:17
Zechariah 2:5
Revelation 20:1–9
- Is the food that feeds our soul

Deuteronomy 8:1–3
Job 23:12
Psalm 119:103–104
Jeremiah 3:15
Jeremiah 15:16
Ezekiel 2:8
Ezekiel 3:4
Matthew 4:1–4
Isaiah 55:2
1 Corinthians 10:3–4
Luke 8:4–15
John 6:1–59

Hebrews 5:1–14
Hebrews 6:5
1 Peter 2:2
Revelation 2:7–17
- To enlighten man's path

Psalm 19:8
Psalm 119:105
Psalm 119:130
Proverbs 6:23
Amos 3:7
Mark 13:23
2 Corinthians 4:6
2 Timothy 3:15–17
Hebrews 1:1–3
2 Peter 1:16–21
2 Peter 3:1–2
- Is the only path to God

Deuteronomy 4:29
2 Chronicles 7:14
Proverbs 8:17
Jeremiah 29:13
Luke 11:9
Leviticus 10:1–3
Deuteronomy 17:14–20
Deuteronomy 28:58–62
- To provide man hope

Romans 15:4
1 John 5:13
- All Scripture is given by God

Jeremiah 36:2
Ezekiel 1:3
Zechariah 7:12
Acts 1:16
Acts 28:25
2 Timothy 3:16
2 Peter 1:21
Revelation 1:1
Revelation 14:13
- Precepts are written in our hearts

Deuteronomy 6:6
Deuteronomy 11:18
Deuteronomy 30:14
Psalm 37:30–34
Psalm 40:8
Psalm 119:11
Jeremiah 31:33
Jeremiah 32:40
Romans 2:15
Romans 7:7–25
Romans 10:8
Colossians 3:16
2 Corinthians 3:3
Hebrews 8:1–13
Hebrews 10:16
Luke 2:51
- God is not the author of confusion

1 Corinthians 14:33
- God's Word will not fail

1 Kings 8:56
Psalm 111:7
Ezekiel 12:25
Daniel 9:12
Matthew 5:18
Luke 21:33
- Nothing in God's Word is coincidental

Exodus 4:10–12
Numbers 11:25
Numbers 23:5
2 Samuel 23:2
1 Kings 22:14
2 Kings 3:11–12
2 Kings 17:13
2 Chronicles 17:9
2 Chronicles 24:20
Nehemiah 8:13
Nehemiah 9:30
Isaiah 50:4
Isaiah 51:16
Jeremiah 1:9–10
Jeremiah 20:9
Jeremiah 36:2
Jeremiah 5:14
Ezekiel 1:3
Ezekiel 3:17
Ezekiel 11:5
Micah 3:8
Zechariah 7:12
Matthew 5:17–18
Matthew 10:19
Luke 21:15
Acts 1:16
Acts 11:28
Acts 21:11

Acts 28:25
1 Corinthians 2:13
1 Corinthians 10:11
2 Timothy 3:16–17
Hebrews 1:1–4
1 Peter 1:11
2 Peter 1:21
2 Peter 3:2
Revelation 1:1
Revelation 14:13

- We are commanded to study God's Word

2 Timothy 2:15
2 Timothy 3:14–17
Exodus 24:7
Leviticus 26:1–13
Deuteronomy 6:1–9
Deuteronomy 17:14–20
Deuteronomy 29:9
Deuteronomy 31:9–13
Joshua 8:30–35
2 Kings 23:1–3
Nehemiah 8:1–18
Isaiah 34:16
Jeremiah 36:6–8
John 5:39
Acts 17:11
Romans 15:4
Colossians 4:16

God holds man accountable to God's Word.

Last words of Jesus on the cross
Mark 15:34
Psalm 22:1

- To the Pharisees

Matthew 12:3–5
Matthew 19:1–12
- To the scribes and high priest

Matthew 21:10–17
- To the Sadducees

Matthew 22:23–33

Peter gave credence to Paul's letters
2 Peter 3:15–16

Jesus gave credence to the Old Testament
Luke 16:29–30

Jesus taught using parables
Psalm 78:2–4
Matthew 13:10–11
Matthew 13:34–35

Jesus is the Word
John 1:1–5
John 5:37–39
2 Corinthians 4:6
Hebrews 10:7
Revelation 1:11–13
Revelation 19:11–13

God's Word lasts forever
Psalm 119:89
Psalm 119:152
Isaiah 40:8
Matthew 5:18
Matthew 24:35
Mark 13:31
1 Peter 1:25

God's Word brings love
Psalm 119:47
Psalm 119:72
Psalm 119:82
Psalm 119:97
Psalm 119:140
Psalm 119:163
Jeremiah 15:16

God told Jeremiah to write the book of Jeremiah
Jeremiah 36:2

God told Moses to write Genesis through Deuteronomy
Exodus 17:8–14
Exodus 24:10–27
Leviticus 18:5
Numbers 33:2
Deuteronomy 31:9
Romans 10:5
Galatians 3:10

The Song of Moses
Deuteronomy 31:22
Deuteronomy 32:44
Revelation 15:5

Old Testament was written to the last generation
1 Corinthians 10:11
Amos 3:7
Daniel 12:1–13
Mark 13:23
Matthew 24:25–26

God's Word is the famine of the end-time
Amos 8:11

God told John to write the book of Revelation
Revelation 1:11

The purpose of Psalms is to give thanks to God
1 Chronicles 16:7–9
- To tell others of God's wonderful works

Psalm 95:1–2
Psalm 105:1–2
- To prophesy about Jesus and to teach others about Jesus

Luke 20:42–44
Luke 24:44
- To provide instruction to the church

Acts 1:20
- To lift up members of the church

Ephesians 5:6–21
Colossians 3:16

God's Word
- Jesus is the Word

John 1:1–5
John 5:37–39
Hebrews 10:7
Revelation 1:11–13
- Is a light in darkness

Psalm 19:8
Psalm 119:105
Psalm 119:130
Proverbs 6:23
2 Corinthians 4:6

2 Peter 1:1–19
- Is a two-edged sword

Hebrews 4:12
Ezekiel 14:17
- Is a devouring flame

Jeremiah 5:14
Jeremiah 23:29
- Is a crushing hammer

Jeremiah 23:29
- Proves what is right and what is wrong

John 20:31
Hebrews 11:1–6
- Ignorance of it is dangerous

Matthew 22:29
John 20:9
Acts 13:27
2 Corinthians 3:15

Precepts are written in the heart
Deuteronomy 6:6
Deuteronomy 11:18
Deuteronomy 30:14
Psalm 119:11
Luke 2:51
Romans 10:8
Colossians 3:16

Nothing written in the Bible is coincidental
2 Chronicles 17:9
Nehemiah 8:13
Matthew 5:17

Matthew 5:18
1 Corinthians 10:11
2 Timothy 3:16–17

God's Word produces faith
Romans 10:17
- is profitable for instruction

Deuteronomy 4:10
Deuteronomy 11:19
2 Chronicles 17:9

We are sanctified through its message
John 17:17
1 Peter 2:2
1 Thessalonians 4:3
Psalm 119:9–11
Proverbs 30:5–6
John 15:7
Acts 20:32

Answers to man's three most important questions
- Where did I come from?

Genesis 1:26–27
Psalm 100:3
- Why am I here?

Ecclesiastes 12:13
Revelation 4:11
- Where am I going?

John 3:16–18
Psalm 23:1
Psalm 23:6
Revelation 20:15

Purpose of Old Testament
Romans 15:4

God's Word was written with a purpose
- To authenticate the divinity of Jesus Christ

John 20:31
- To give hope to men

Romans 15:4
- To give knowledge of eternal life

1 John 5:13
- To purify lives

Psalm 119:9
John 15:3
John 17:17
Ephesians 5:26
1 Peter 1:22

The standard of faith and duty
Proverbs 29:18
Isaiah 8:20
John 12:48
Galatians 1:8
1 Thessalonians 2:13

The Word is scared, not to be altered
Deuteronomy 4:2
Deuteronomy 12:32
Proverbs 30:6
Revelation 22:19

We are commanded to study
Deuteronomy 17:19

Isaiah 34:16
John 5:39
Acts 17:11
Romans 15:4
2 Timothy 2:15
Joshua 1:8
Matthew 4:4

Contains seed for sowing
Psalm 126:6
Mark 4:14–15
2 Corinthians 9:10

Absolutely trustworthy
1 Kings 8:56
Psalm 93:5
Psalm 111:7
Ezekiel 12:25
Daniel 9:12
Matthew 5:18
Romans 4:6

Jesus foretold us all things
Mark 13:23

God's word reveals all things to man
Amos 3:7
Mark 13:23
2 Peter 1:16–21
2 Peter 3:1–2
Hebrews 1:1–3
Matthew 24:25–26

God's Word will last through all time
Psalm 119:89
Isaiah 40:8

Matthew 5:18
Matthew 24:38
1 Peter 1:25

Why Jesus spoke in parables
Matthew 13:10–11

God's Word is our true food
Deuteronomy 8:3
Matthew 4:4
Job 23:12
Psalm 119:103
Jeremiah 3:15
Jeremiah 15:16
Ezekiel 2:8–10
Ezekiel 3:1–4
John 6:32–58
Hebrews 6:5
1 Peter 2:2
Revelation 2:7–17

Must read Bible in context
Isaiah 28:10–13
2 Timothy 2:15

Example of not reading in context
John 3:26
John 4:2

God is judge
Psalm 75:7

God judges no man
John 5:22–27

Jesus quotes
Luke 4:12
Deuteronomy 6:16

Jesus is the Word
John 1:1–5
John 5:37–39
Hebrews 10:7
Revelation 19:11–13

Faith comes by hearing, hearing by God's Word
Romans 10:17

Must hear, understand, and do God's Word
Deuteronomy 4:1–14

What God will do to the wicked
Psalm 37:7
Psalm 37:20
Psalm 37:34

Some are blinded to God's Word by God
Romans 11:25

Can only come to God through God's Word
Leviticus 29:9–29
Deuteronomy 28:58–62
Deuteronomy 17:18

The Word accuses the unsaved to God
John 5:37–47

Satan uses the Word against us
Matthew 4:1–7

Moses wrote the Torah
Exodus 17:14
Exodus 24:7
Numbers 5:23
Deuteronomy 29:21
Deuteronomy 31:22–26

Old Testament is example for today
Romans 15:4
1 Corinthians 10:11

Water = People
Hebrews 12:
Revelation 1:7
Revelation 17:15
Revelation 20:13

Sadducees err because of not reading
Matthew 22:23–29

Why read God's Word
Colossians 1:2

You receive peace when you read the Word of God
All Scripture was given by the spirit of God
2 Peter 1:20–21
2 Timothy 3:15–17
2 Timothy 2:15–16
Jeremiah 36:2
Ezekiel 1:3
Zechariah 7:12
Acts 1:6
Revelation 1:1
Revelation 14:13

The law of the Lord is perfect converting the soul
Psalm 19:7–11

The Word of the Lord is tried and true
2 Samuel 22:31
Psalm 12:6

The Word of the Lord cleanses
Psalm 19:9

The Word of the Lord gives eternal life
Acts 19:18–20
Psalm 119:50
Ezekiel 37:7
Romans 1:16
Romans 10:13–17
Matthew 16:13–20

The Word of the Lord can work quickly
Psalm 147:15

Jesus warned the scribes and Pharisees concerning their illiteracy of the Scriptures
Matthew 12:3–5
Matthew 19:1–12

Jesus warned the high priest concerning their illiteracy
Matthew 21:10–17

Jesus warned the Sadducees concerning their illiteracy as well
Matthew 22:23–33

The Word of the Lord is the sword of the Spirit
Ephesians 6:17
Matthew 4:1–11

Prophecy
Prophecy of Esau and Jacob
Genesis chapters 25–27
Prophets' commands
1 Samuel 1:17
1 Kings 17:13
2 Kings 3:16
2 Kings 4:3, 7
2 Kings 5:10

Voice of the prophets
Matthew 13:35
Matthew 21:4
Luke 1:70
Acts 3:21
James 5:10
2 Peter 3:2

Inspiration of prophets comes from God
2 Kings 3:11–12
2 Kings 17:13
Nehemiah 9:30
Hebrews 1:1
1 Peter 1:11
2 Peter 1:20–21

What false prophets do to real prophets
1 Kings 12:25
1 Kings 13:32

Jesus said to read Genesis (days of Noah) to see Second Coming
Matthew 24:37
Genesis 6
Genesis 10

Jesus said to read Daniel to see event of the end
Matthew 24:15
Daniel 9:25–27

Jesus was prophesied to come First Coming as King, and double prophecy showed his Second Coming as King
Matthew 21:4–5
Zechariah 9:9–10

Jesus taught to interpret Scripture symbolically using metaphors
Luke 9:57–62

Jesus taught us to search for double references in prophecy
Luke 4:14–21
Isaiah 61:1–5

By reading this Scripture in church, Jesus was teaching to interpret Scripture literally
Luke 4:14–21
Isaiah 61:1–5

Jesus fulfilled the prophets
Matthew 2:15

Paul taught to read God's Word in church
Colossians 4:16

The Word

God is not the author of confusion
1 Corinthians 14:33

Middle chapter of the Bible
Psalm 118

LOVE IS

Shortest chapter
Psalm 117

Longest chapter
Psalm 119

"Word" appears 42 times
42 = Lord's Advent
6 × 7 = 42
6 = man's number 7 = complete

"Law" appears 25 times
25 = forgiveness of sin

"Testimonies" appears 23 times
23 = death

"Precepts" appears 21 times
21 = exceeding swiftness of sin

"God's Statutes" appears 22 times
22 = light

"God's commandments" appears 22 times

"God's judgement" appears 22 times

Jews taught to interpret verses symbolically
Luke 9:57–62

Jesus taught to interpret verses literally
Luke 4:14–21

Scripture lawyers
Luke 11

Feed the meat of the Word
Hebrews 5

The Word
The Pentateuch: Torah
Jesus gave credence to the Old Testament
Luke 16:29–31

Pentateuch
Torah is Genesis through Deuteronomy
Moses wrote the Torah
Exodus 24:1–4
Exodus 34:10–27

God told Moses to write Exodus
Exodus 17:8–14

Moses wrote Leviticus
Leviticus 18:5
Romans 10:5

Moses wrote Numbers
Numbers 33:2

Moses wrote Deuteronomy
Deuteronomy 31:9

Song of Moses
Deuteronomy 31:22
Deuteronomy 32:44
Revelation 15:5

God commanded us to teach our children his Word
Deuteronomy 6:4–12
Deuteronomy 17:14–20

The Torah
Joshua 1:7–8
Joshua 8:31–32
1 Kings 2:3
2 Kings 14:6
2 Kings 21:8
Ezra 6:18
Nehemiah 13:1
Daniel 9:11–13
Malachi 4:4
Matthew 19:8
Mark 12:26
John 1:45
John 5:46–47
Acts 3:22
Romans 10:5
Luke 24:27–44

Jesus told us we are clean through the Word
John 15:3

How Satan changes God's Word
Psalm 91:11–12
Matthew 4:5–7

Need for meat of the Word
Hebrews 5
Hebrews 6

Nothing new under the sun
Ecclesiastes 1

New earth 1
Isaiah 65
Contradiction?
Answer: Now in Spirit body, no longer in flesh body
Isaiah 66

Prayer—use of tongues
Acts 1:1:8
Tower of Babel
Genesis 11:1–4

God created by the power of his Word
Psalm 33:6–9
Israel is an olive tree
Jeremiah 11:16

Mysteries

Must have eyes that see and ears to hear to understand the mysteries of God
Matthew 13:11–18

To understand mysteries, one must first understand the Parable of the Sower
Mark 4:1–13
Matthew 13:11–18

Mysteries are given in parables
Luke 8:1–10
Matthew 13:11–18

The fact that God shut the eyes of Israel is a mystery
Romans 11:25–26

The mystery of Jesus was kept secret since the world began
Romans 16:25

LOVE IS

1 Corinthians 2:7
Ephesians 3:1–9

There are many mysteries
1 Corinthians 4:1

Love is greater than understanding all mysteries
1 Corinthians 13:1–13

The duty of ones that understand mysteries
1 Corinthians 13:1
1 Corinthians 14:40

The fact that we return to God when our physical bodies die is a mystery
1 Corinthians 15:51

The will of God is a mystery
Ephesians 1:9

The true church is a mystery
Ephesians 5:32

The gospel is a mystery
Ephesians 6:19

Jesus dwelling in us is a mystery
Colossians 1:26–27

Jesus being our Savior is a mystery
Colossians 2:1–9
Colossians 4:3
Psalm 25:4–5
Psalm 25:14

Iniquity is a mystery
2 Thessalonians 2:7

Faith is a mystery
1 Timothy 3:9

Godliness is a mystery
1 Timothy 3:16

The stars in Jesus's right hand are a mystery
Revelation 1:20

All mysteries will end at Jesus's return
Revelation 10:7
Mark 4:22
Luke 8:17

Babylon is a mystery
Revelation 17:5
Revelation 17:7

Mysteries belong to God
Deuteronomy 29:29
Psalm 81:7
Psalm 90:1
Ezekiel 7:22

The name of Jesus is a secret (mystery)
Judges 13:18

Secret faults
Psalm 19:12
Psalm 90:8

God's protection is a mystery
Psalm 31:24

The wicked plan in secret
Psalm 64:1–6
Ephesians 5:12
Habakkuk 3:14
Psalm 83:1–3

Truth is hidden from the wicked
Proverbs 9:17
Lamentations 3:10
Revelation 2:17

God knows all secrets
Ecclesiastes 12:14
Isaiah 45:1–3
Jeremiah 23:24
Jeremiah 49:10
Psalm 44:21
Romans 2:16
Obadiah 6
1 Corinthians 4:5

God cries in secret places
Jeremiah 13:17

God reveals secrets
Daniel 2:1–47
1 Corinthians 4:5
Revelation 2:17
Daniel 4:1–37
Amos 3:7
Psalm 51:6
Isaiah 48:6

Jesus told us to pray in secret
Matthew 6:6
Matthew 6:4–18

God's Word is a mystery
Revelation 2:17

All have sinned
2 Chronicles 6:36

We are sealed in Jesus
Ephesians 4:30
Ephesians 1:3–14

God created with the power of his Word
Psalm 33:6–9

Israel is an olive tree
Jeremiah 11:16

God did not turn his back on Jesus
John 8:29
John 10:17
John 10:30
John 14:6–12
John 14:19–21
John 16:29–32
Matthew 26:51–54

Pride was downfall of Satan
Psalm 10:2
Psalm 10:4
Psalm 10:6

The Holy Spirit lives in us
John 14:15–17
Matthew 10:19–20

Old Testament Statistics

39 books
- 929 chapters
- 23,214 verses
- 593,495 words
- Longest book—Psalms
- Shortest book—Obadiah
- 17 historical books
- 5 poetical books
- 17 prophetical books

New Testament Statistics
- 27 books
- 260 chapters
- 9,959 verses
- 181,253 words longest book—Acts
- Shortest book—2 John
- 4 gospels
- 1 historical
- 22 epistles

Facts about Job
- Birth of Job (Genesis 46:13)
- God was very pleased with Job (Job 1:6–12)
- Job is accused of being in sin (Job 4:7)
- God is blamed for Job's condition (Job 4:9)
- Job's friend claiming to be a prophet (Job 4:12)
- Job still did not sin (Job 1:21–22)
- Seven days' silence before Job's friends begin (Job 2:11–13)
- Job gives his complaint (Job 3:1–26)
- Job defends himself (chapters 4–31)
- Elihu enters discussion (chapters 32–37)
- God said Job's friends darken council (Job 38:2)

We were with God when he created earth (Job 38:1–7, Job 40:15)
You reap what you sow (Galatians 6:7)
God chose you (Deuteronomy 10:15)
Your spirit returns to God (Ecclesiastes 12:7)
God does talk with man (Deuteronomy 5:24)
God does speak (Isaiah 52:6)
God collects our tears in a bottle (Psalm 56:8)
Lift up your hands in church (Psalm 134:2)
God sets members in body of Christ (1 Corinthians 12:18)
There is neither male nor female in God's body of Christians (Galatians 3:28)
It may be that you will be hidden in the day of the Lord's wrath (Zephaniah 2:3)
The Second Coming of the Lord Jesus Christ (Mark chapter 13)
God creates evil (Isaiah 45:7)
Dogs go to heaven (Psalm 36:6)
Book of Life (Revelation 20:12)
God is not angry with us (Isaiah 54:9)
Those who will not inherit the kingdom of God (1 Corinthians 6:9)
End-times (Luke 21:26)
Only true God (John 17:3)
God knows you (Psalm 139:13–16)
On homosexuals (1 Corinthians 6:9–11)
Only way to God is Jesus Christ (John 14:6)
Baptized with the Holy Spirit (Acts 11:16)
Spoke with tongues and prophesied (Acts 19:6)
Gifts of the Holy Spirit (1 Corinthians 12:7–11)
Casting out spirits (John 3:3)

Book of Esther
Jesus is our advocate
God will deliver his children

LOVE IS

Book of Job
Jesus is our redeemer
God delivers the suffering righteous

Book of Psalms
Jesus is our all in all
The book of Jewish songs

Book of Proverbs
Jesus is our wisdom
God gives wisdom to his children

Book of Ecclesiastes
Jesus is the beginning and the end
The book of the preacher

Book of the Song of Solomon
Jesus is the lover of our soul
God loves, so we are to love God

Jesus will come to all that seek him (Matthew 7:7–11)
Jesus is the cleaner of sin (1 John 1:7–10)
Jesus was sent by the will of God, not man (Genesis 3:15, John 1:13, John 4:31–34)
Jesus is the Lamb of God (John 1:29, Exodus 12, Genesis 22, John 1:29–37)
Jesus is the judge (John 5:22–27)
Jesus kept the Passover (John 6:1–13)
Jesus, as seen by the masses (Luke 11:14–36)
Jesus was thirty years old when he began his ministry (Luke 3:1–23, Ezekiel 1:1, Numbers 4:1–3)
Jesus came preaching peace (Ephesians 2:15–17)
Jesus is the only way to salvation (John 3:16–18, John 6:26–35, John 7:37–38, John 10:1–18)
Jesus replaced Old Covenant with the New Covenant (Hebrews 10:1–9)

Jesus appeared to Daniel (Daniel 10:5–10)
Jesus is the same yesterday, today, and tomorrow (Hebrews 13:8)
We are saved for Jesus's name's sake (1 John 2:12, Isaiah 43:25)
God did not destroy Israel for God's name's sake (Numbers 14:11–24)
Jesus was in the linage of priests (Psalm 104:4, Hebrews 5:5–6)
Jesus was in the linage of kings (Luke 1:32–33)
Jesus taught us how to pray (Matthew 6:5–15)
Jesus was the helper of the sick and possessed (Matthew 4:23–25)
Jesus was called a Nazarene (Matthew 2:19–23)
Jesus is Emmanuel—God with us (Matthew 11:23)
Jesus was commanded to give his life (John 10:14–18)
Jesus is creator of all things (Colossians 1:16–17)
Jesus came to save (John 3:16–17, 1 Peter 3:18–20, Matthew 1:21)
Jesus is the will of our Father (John 6:38–40)
Jesus is Son of Man (Luke 5:24, John 1:43–51, John 2:1–25)
Jesus is the Son of God (John 1:14–18, John 1:29–34, John 3:16, 1 John 4:9, Matthew 13:16–17, Matthew 17:1–2)
Jesus and our Father are one (John 14:1–11, Matthew 1:23)
Jesus is the divider (Matthew 25:31–34, Genesis 1:4–14)
Jesus spoke in parables, why? (Matthew 13:10–11)
Jesus is the Word (John 1:1–3, 2 Corinthians 4:6, Revelation 19:11–13, Hebrews 10:7)
Jesus is the light (John 1:4–5, Isaiah 9:1–2, John 9:1–5, Genesis 1:3, 2 Corinthians 4:6, Matthew 4:12–16)
Jesus came to his own, and they knew him not (John 1:11)
John the Baptist witnessed Jesus as "The Light" (John 1:6–9)
All that come to Jesus are saved and are born of God (John 1:12–13, 1 John 2:29)
Apostle John knew Jesus and beheld Jesus's glory (John 1:14)
John the Baptist and the Apostles witnessed of Jesus and received grace (John 1:15–16)
Grace came by Jesus, and law came by Moses (John 1:17)
No man has seen God; Jesus has declared God to men (John 1:18)

John the Baptist, speaking of himself, told who he was (John 1:19–28)

John the Baptist, speaking to the Pharisees, told them they did not know Jesus (John 1:24–28)

How John the Baptist knew who Jesus was (John 1:29–34)

Why Jesus came to earth (Matthew 18:10–14, Romans 10, Matthew 9:13, Isaiah 49, Luke 4:14–21)

Why Jesus being rejected at his first coming was part of God's plan (John 1:8–11, Isaiah 53:3, John 6:38–40, John 17:2–4, Isaiah 61:1–5)

Jesus is the Tree of Life (Proverbs 13:12, Revelation 22:2, Genesis 2:9, Hosea 14:8)

Jesus preached to souls born before him (1 Peter 3:18–19, Ephesians 4)

Jesus is the rock, the foundation stone, the cornerstone (Deuteronomy 13:50, Numbers 20:11–13, Psalm 31:3, Psalm 71:1–3, Matthew 7:24–27, Romans 9:33, Isaiah 28:16, 1 Corinthians 10:4)

Jesus walked through a wall in his spiritual body (John 19:20–26)

Jesus's first Advent (Zachariah 9:9)

Jesus's second Advent (Zachariah 9:10)

Jesus is our high priest (Hebrews 5)

Jesus is the living water (John 4:1–9, Isaiah 12:1–3, Isaiah 49:8–11, Revelation 7:12–17)

Jesus was with God in the first earth age (John 17:5–24)

God is not a respecter of persons (Deuteronomy 1:1–18, Ephesians 6:9, Colossians 3:23–26)

Details the death of Jesus on the cross (Psalm 22)

Jesus is the door to life (John 10:9)

Jesus has the key to heaven (Matthew 16:13–20)

Jesus has the key to the kingdom of death (Revelation 1:18)

The fame of Jesus was spread into the entire world (Colossians 1:1–6, Matthew 24:14)

Jesus created all things and is above all things (Colossians 7:29, John 1:13)

The Lord is my shepherd: I shall not want. He maketh me to lie down in green pastures; he leadeth me beside the still waters. He restoreth my soul: He leadeth me in paths of righteousness for his names sake. Yea, though I walk through the valley of the shadow of death, I will fear on evil, for thou art with me; thy rod and thy staff, they comfort me. Thou preparest a table before me in the presence of mine enemies: thou anointest my head with oil: my cup runneth over. Surely goodness and mercy shall follow me all the days of my life: and I will dwell in the house of the Lord forever. (Psalm 23)

Events seen by the prophets

The Antichrist (Isaiah 14:4–20, Daniel 7:19–27, Ezekiel 28:11–19, Zechariah 11:15–17, Revelation 13:1–8)

The Great Tribulation (Joel 2:1–11, Isaiah 2:19–21, Isaiah 26:20–21, Daniel 21:1, Revelation 16:1–21)

Armageddon (Joel 3:1–17, Isaiah 11:4–5, Isaiah 63:1–6, Zephaniah 3:8, Ezekiel 39:1–28, Zechariah 14:1–3, Revelation 19:17–21)

Jesus's Second Coming (Daniel 7:9–14, Zechariah 12:7–14, Zechariah 14:4–11, Malachi 3:1–3, Malachi 4:1–6, Revelation 19:11–16)

The millennium—Jesus's one-thousand-year reign (Joel 2:21–27, Joel 3:18–21, Amos 9:13–15, Micah 4:1–7, Isaiah 35:1–10, Isaiah 11:4–10, Isaiah 2:2–4, Zephaniah 3:20, Habakkuk 2:14, Jeremiah 31:27–34, Jeremiah 33:12–26, Ezekiel 36:33–36, Ezekiel 40:1–4, Ezekiel 8:35, Haggai 2:6–9, Zachariah 8:3–4, Zachariah 14:16–21, Revelation 20:7–10)

Earth burned by fire (Revelation 20:1, Revelation 21:1, 2 Peter 3:5–13)

New Heaven, New Earth, and New Jerusalem (Isaiah 60:18–22, Isaiah 65:17, Isaiah 66:22, Revelation 21:1, Revelation 22:5)

Things God hates (Proverbs 6, Matthew 15:19)

Trees of Lebanon are cedar—cedar trees are evergreen trees (Judges 9:8, Isaiah 60:25, Isaiah 61:37)

God owns all souls (Psalm 82:6, Ezekiel 18:4, John 10:34, Ecclesiastes 12:6–7, 2 Corinthians 5:6–8)

God wants our love (1 Samuel 15:22, Matthew 9:13, Psalm 40:6)

Wisdom of God (Proverbs 8:22–30)

Divorced Israel (Jeremiah 3:8–14, 1 Corinthians 7)

Got married (Ezekiel 16:8, Isaiah 54:5)

God owns everything (Job 41:11, Romans 11:35, 1 Corinthians 8:6, 1 Corinthians 11:12)

God is a consuming fire (Leviticus 9:24, Genesis 15:17, Exodus 3:1–6, 1 Kings 18–38, Habakkuk 12:29, Hebrew 12:29, Luke 12:49)

God created man for his pleasure (Revelation 4:11)

God is from everlasting to everlasting (Psalm 135:13, Hebrews 7:1–3, Deuteronomy 32:39–40, Deuteronomy 33:27)

The work of God (John 6:24–71, Amos 3:7, Colossians 3:25–26)

God is love (1 John 4:16)

One day with God is as one thousand with man (2 Peter 3:8)

The light of the knowledge of the glory of God in the face of Jesus Christ (2 Corinthians 4:6)

God loves us even in our sins (Romans 5:6–8)

God never sleeps (Matthew 18:10, Isaiah 40:18–31, Psalm 121)

God never turns his back on his children (Psalm 22:1, Matthew 15:34, Matthew 27:46, Ezekiel 28, Job 1)

Jesus and our Father are one (John 14:1–11, Matthew 1:23)

God speaks to man from inside man (Ephesians 4:4–6)

God is at war with Satan, not man (Exodus 15:3)

God did not destroy Israel for his name's sake (Numbers 14:11–24, Ezekiel 20:7–10, Ezekiel 20:19–22)

We are saved for Jesus's name's sake (1 John 2:12, Isaiah 43:25)
The war with Satan was started by Satan's rebellion (Jeremiah 4:19–31, Isaiah 14, Ezekiel 28)
God destroyed the first earth age (Genesis 1:2, Jeremiah 4:23–26, Hebrews 12:25–27, 2 Peter 3:5–6)
God fights the war with Satan, not us (Psalm 110:1, 2 Chronicles 20:1–17, 1 Samuel 17:47)
The army of God (2 Kings 6:17)
The blessing of God (Numbers 6:22)

Obedience is the key to the kingdom of godliness.

Attributes of God

God is omnipresent (Deuteronomy 4:39, Psalm 139:8, Proverbs 15:3, Isaiah 66:1, Jeremiah 23:24, Acts 17:27, Zechariah 2:5, Job 26:6, Job 31:4, Job 34:21, Psalm 147:5, Hebrews 4:13, 1 John 3:20)
Nearness of God (Psalm 16:8, Psalm 34:18, Psalm 119:151, Psalm 145:18, Jeremiah 23:23, Acts 17:27)
God does not change (Psalm 33:11, Psalm 102:27, Malachi 3:6, Hebrews 1:12, Hebrews 13:8, James 1:17, Proverbs 19:21, Isaiah 14:27, Isaiah 25:1, Isaiah 46:10, Jeremiah 4:28, Daniel 4:35, Acts 5:39, Ephesians 1:11, Hebrews 6:17)
God is eternal (Deuteronomy 32:40, Deuteronomy 33:27, Psalm 9:7, Psalm 135:13, Psalm 145:13, Isaiah 57:15, Lamentations 5:19, 2 Peter 3:8, Revelation 1:8, Revelation 11:17, Isaiah 9:7, Daniel 2:44, Daniel 4:3, Daniel 4:3, Daniel 4:34, Daniel 6:28, Daniel 7:13–14, Luke 1:32–33, 2 Peter 1:11, Revelation 11:15, Psalm 90:2, Micah 5:2, Hebrews 7:1–3)
God's will is that all be saved (2 Peter 3:9, Ezekiel 33:10–11, Matthew 9:10, Matthew 12:6–12, Luke 12:41, John 8:42, John 17:14)
God is love (1 John 4:8)

LOVE IS

All the law is fulfilled in one word: *love* (Romans 5:20, Matthew 5:17–20, Matthew 7:12, Romans 3:10, 1 John 3:23–24, 1 John 4:7–21, Galatians 5:14, 1 Timothy 1:5, 1 John 2:7–11, Matthew 7:12, Proverbs 10:12)

Seven things God hates

Matthew 15:19—(1) evil thoughts, (2) murders, (3) adulteries, (4) fornication, (5) thefts, (6) false witness, (7) blasphemies

Proverbs 6:16—(1) a proud look, (2) lying tongue, (3) hands that shed innocent blood, (4) wicked imaginations, (5) swift running to mischief, (6) false witness, (7) sow discord among brethren

God is a consuming fire (Leviticus 9:24, 1 Kings 18:38, Genesis 15:17, Exodus 3:1–6, Hebrews 12:29)

God is power (1 Chronicles 29:12, 2 Chronicles 25:8, Job 26:12, Psalm 62:11, Psalm 65:6, Psalm 93:4, Romans 16:25–27, Genesis 15:1)

God is

- able to deliver (Daniel 3:17),
- able to raise up children from stone (Luke 3:8),
- able to fulfill promises (Romans 4:21),
- able to make grace abound (2 Corinthians 9:8),
- able to do exceeding abundantly above all we can ask or think (Ephesians 3:20),
- able to subdue all things (Philippians 3:21),
- able to guard the souls treasure (2 Timothy 1:12),
- able to save to the uttermost (Hebrews 7:25),
- able to keep us from falling (Jude 24).

God uses weak things to accomplish great things (2 Corinthians 12)
A rod (Exodus 4:2)
A jawbone (Judges 15:15)
Five smooth stones (1 Samuel 17:40)
A handful of flour and a little oil (1 Kings 17:12)
A cloud the size of a man's hand (1 Kings 18:44)
Small things (Zechariah 4:10)
A mustard seed (Matthew 13:32)
Five barley loaves (John 6:9)
God's instrument case (1 Corinthians 1:27–29)

God has power over nature
Multiplying the loaves (Matthew 14:20)
Walking on the sea (Matthew 14:25)
Discovering the tribute money (Matthew 17:27)
Cursing the fig tree (Matthew 21:19)
Stilling the tempest (Jonah 1:15, Matthew 8:26, Mark 4:39, Psalm 65:7, Psalm 89:8, Psalm 107:29)
Turning water into wine (John 2:7)
Setting boundaries for the seas (Job 38:8–11, Psalm 33:7, Psalm 104:9, Proverbs 8:29, Jeremiah 5:22)
Ruling the wind (Psalm 148:8, Proverbs 30:4, Mark 4:39)

For God so loved the world (John 3:16)

God's True Nature

God protects and loves his children: would not allow his children to fight the war of rebellion started by Satan (John 3:16, Genesis 15:1)
God is love (1 John 4:8, Romans 5:20, Romans 3:10, Matthew 5:17–20, Matthew 7:12, 1 John 3:23–24, 1 John 2:7–11, Galatians 5:14, 1 Timothy 1:5, Proverbs 10:12)
God is full of understanding, knowledge, and wisdom (Proverbs 8:22–30)

God is glory (2 Corinthians 4:6)
God is a redeemer (Galatians 4:4–5)
God is a consuming fire (Leviticus 9:24, Genesis 15:17, Exodus 3:1–6, 1 Kings 18:38, Hebrews 12:29, Luke 12:49)
God compares himself to an eagle (Exodus 19:4)
God compares himself to a fir tree (Hosea 14:8)
Trees of Lebanon are cedar and fir (1 Kings 5:5–10)
Omniscience of God—knows all things (John 2:24, John 16:30, John 21:17, Acts 1:24, Job 26:6, Job 31:4, Job 34:21, Psalm 147:5, Hebrews 4:13, 1 John 3:20, 1 Samuel 2:3, Psalm 69:5, Psalm 139:2, Isaiah 40:28, Daniel 2:22, Matthew 6:8, 1 Corinthians 3:20, 1 John 3:20, Isaiah 11:2, Matthew 13:54, Luke 2:40, 1 Corinthians 1:24, Colossians 2:3)
God's wisdom (Proverbs 8:22–30)
Wisdom of the world or worldly wisdom shall be destroyed (Isaiah 29:14, Jeremiah 4:22, Ezekiel 28:4, Romans 1:22, 1 Corinthians 1:19, 1 Corinthians 2:6, 1 Corinthians 3:19–20, 2 Corinthians 1:12, Colossians 2:23, James 3:15, Psalm 49:13, Proverbs 14:8, Proverbs 15:14, Proverbs 18:13, Proverbs 26:11, Ecclesiastes 2:13, Ecclesiastes 10:1)

Characteristics of fools

Atheism (Psalm 53:1)
Slander (Proverbs 10:18)
Mocking sin (Proverbs 14:9)
Despising instruction (Proverbs 15:5)
Contentious (Proverbs 18:6)
Meddlesome (Proverbs 20:3)
Self-confident (Proverbs 28:26, Ecclesiastes 7:9)
Dishonest (Jeremiah 17:11, Matthew 7:26)
Hypocrite (Luke 11:39–40, Romans 1:22, Ephesians 5:15)
Deceived (Proverbs 1:22, Proverbs 7:7, Proverbs 8:5, Proverbs 14:15, Proverbs 22:3, Hosea 7:11)
Manifest foolishness (Proverbs 12:23, Proverbs 15:2, Proverbs 18:2, Ecclesiastes 5:3, Ecclesiastes 10:3, 2 Timothy 3:9)

Conceited (Proverbs 3:7, Proverbs 26:5, Proverbs 26:12, Isaiah 5:21, Romans 12:16, 1 Corinthians 8:2, Galatians 6:3)

Philosophy (Acts 17:18, 1 Corinthians 1:19, 1 Corinthians 2:6, Colossians 2:8)

God knows the sin of man (Jeremiah 2:22, Jeremiah 16:17, Ezekiel 11:5, Hosea 7:2)

God knows the hearts of man (1 Chronicles 28:9, Jeremiah 17:10, Jeremiah 23:24, Amos 9:3, Zephaniah 1:12, Romans 8:27, Jeremiah 20:12, Proverbs 15:11, Matthew 12:25, Matthew 22:18, Mark 2:8, Luke 6:8, Luke 11:17, Luke 16:15, John 2:25, Acts 15:8)

Foreknowledge of God (Isaiah 42:9, Isaiah 46:10, Matthew 4:36, Daniel 2:28, Acts 3:18, Acts 15:18, Romans 8:29, Romans 11:2, 1 Peter 1:2)

God's predestination, elect (Proverbs 16:4, Acts 4:28, Romans 8:29, Romans 9:11, Ephesians 1:4, Ephesians 3:11, 1 Peter 1:20, Matthew 24:22, Matthew 24:31, Luke 18:7, Romans 8:33, 2 Timothy 2:10, 1 Peter 1:2, Deuteronomy 7:6, Psalm 4:3, 1 Corinthians 1:26, James 2:5, 1 Peter 2:10, Exodus 6:7, Deuteronomy 4:37, Deuteronomy 7:6, Matthew 25:34, John 15:16, Galatians 4:30)

God told Jesus, "Sit at my right hand until I make thine enemies thy foot stool" (Hebrews 1:13, Hebrews 10:13)

Enemies of Jesus (Matthew 22:44, Mark 12:36, Luke 20:43, Acts 2:35)

Jesus said the footstool of God is the earth (Matthew 5:35)

God made Jesus's enemies his footstool (Psalm 110:1)

God's footstool at the foot of the throne (2 Chronicles 9:18)

God said the earth is his footstool (Acts 7:49)

The Holy Spirit or Holy Ghost

God is the father of spirits (Hebrews 12:9)

God's spirit will not always strive with man (Genesis 6:3)

God teaches through the spirit (1 John 5:6–10, Revelation 1:10, Revelation 2:7, Revelation 2:11, Revelation 2:17, Revelation 2:29, Revelation 3:6, Revelation 3:13, Revelation 3:22, Revelation 4:2, Revelation 14:13, Revelation 17:3, Revelation 19:10, Revelation 21:10, Revelation 29:17, Ephesians 4:4–6)

God protected man in the spirit (Genesis 15:1, Genesis 1:2–5)

We can only worship God in the spirit (John 4:23–24, John 6:63, Romans 1:4–9)

The spirit is truth (1 John 4:6, 1 John 5:6)

Live for God in the spirit (1 Peter 4:6)

The spirit of God came on Jesus (Matthew 3:16, Mark 1:10)

Jesus carried by the spirit (Matthew 4:1, Mark 1:12)

The spirit cast out devils (Matthew 12:28)

Spirit is willing; the flesh is weak (Matthew 26:41)

We rejoice in the spirit (Luke 1:47, Luke 10:21)

We get strong in the spirit (Luke 1:80)

At death, our spirit goes to God (Luke 23:46)

Man must be born in the spirit (John 3:5–8)

The spirit has no flesh and bones (Luke 24:37–39)

The Holy Spirit brings things to our remembrance (John 14)

Work of the Holy Spirit (John 5:32, John 16:13–15, John 16:8–10, John 6:23–71, Ephesians 4:4–6)

Dove represents the Holy Spirit (Matthew 3:16)

The wind represents the Holy Spirit (Genesis 2:7, Ezekiel 37:4–14, Acts 1:1–8, Revelation 7)

The Holy Spirit seals the saved (Revelation 7, Ephesians 4:30)

Jesus sent the Holy Spirit (John 16:1–7, Genesis 2:18, Genesis 3:8–9, Matthew 16:13–17, John 5:31–47, John 6:44–65, John 10:1–30, Ephesians 4:4–6)

The Holy Spirit enters you and testifies to you and calls you to salvation (1 John 5:10)

We are baptized into the Holy Spirit (1 Corinthians 12:13)

The Holy Spirit did not dwell with every true believer until Pentecost was coming (Acts 1:1–2, Matthew 4:19–22, Matthew 16:13–20, 1 John 2:29, Jeremiah 1:4–10)

The elect receive Holy Spirit and assignment before their birth (Luke 1:1–45)
Seventy men received the Holy Spirit and prophesied (Numbers 11:16–35)

Miscellaneous Facts

For everything there is a time and a season (Ecclesiastes 3:1–8)
Unforgivable sin (Luke 12:10)
Behemoth (Job 40:15–19)
All souls came down from heaven and return when they die (John 3:13, Ecclesiastes 12:6–7)
Olive oil anointing (James 5)
The ten commandments (Exodus 20)
Sin is the poison of Satan (1 John 3:4, Deuteronomy 32:33)
How our bodies get with old age (Ecclesiastes 12)
Paul was of the tribe of Benjamin: see blessings of the twelve sons of Jacob (Romans 11:1, Genesis 49)
All meat is clean (1 Timothy 4:4)
Paul taught on three levels (Acts 9:15)
The grafting in of Gentiles (Romans 11)
There is nothing that shall not be known: one-thousand-year reign (Luke 12:2, John 15:26)
God calls us friends (John 15:15)
Adam is the figure of Jesus (Romans 5:10–15)
Solomon, the wisest man on earth (1 Kings 4:29–34)
One day with God is as one thousand with man (2 Peter 3:8)
Water represents man (Hebrews 12:1, Revelation 17:15, Revelation 20:13, Revelation 1:7)
Man is appointed once to be born—no reincarnation (Hebrews 9:27–28)
The same things happen to the good and the evil (Ecclesiastes 9:1–2)
Lightening (Exodus 19:16, 2 Samuel 22:15, Job 37:3, Job 38:35, Psalm 18:14, Nahum 2:4, Revelation 4:5, Matthew 24:27)

LOVE IS

America = ten northern tribes of Israel (Isaiah 18)
Manna is angels' food; manna meaning—what is it? (Psalm 78:24–25)
The righteous shall not be visited with evil (Proverbs 19:23)
God has ordained all nations (Romans 13)
God does not punish the sons for their fathers' sins (Exodus 20:5)
The wine of Satan is poison (Deuteronomy 32:33)
Scrip = a shepherd's bag (1 Samuel 17:40)
God did not heal Paul's physical body (2 Corinthians 12:1–21)
God owns all souls (Psalm 82:1–8, John 3:9–12, Matthew 22:23–33, John 10:34, Ezekiel 18:4, Luke 20:27–40, Luke 16)
Things God hates (Proverbs 6, Matthew 15:19)
Jesus taught us how to pray (Matthew 6:5–15)
Why Jesus spoke in parables (Matthew 13:10–11)
Pharisees do not know God (John 1:24–28)
No man has seen God (John 1:18)
The world does not know Jesus (John 1:10–11)
God owns everything (Job 41:10–11, Romans 11:35, 1 Corinthians 8:6, 1 Corinthians 11:12)
Homosexuality is an abomination (Leviticus 18:22)
Ten men received the Holy Spirit and prophesied (Numbers 11:14–35)
The opposite of the beatitudes (Matthew 23)
God can read our hearts and minds (1 Chronicles 28:9)
The trees of Lebanon are cedar and fir (1 Kings 5:5–10)
Cursed be the man that turns his back on God and trusts in man (Jeremiah 17:5)
People that say God put a burden on his people (Jeremiah 23:33–40)

Love is never bringing up what you have forgiven

God wants our love (Hosea 6:6, Matthew 9:13, 1 Samuel 15:22, Psalm 40:6)

God cares for us (Psalm 115:12, Matthew 6:32, Luke 12:7, 1 Peter 5:7)

God holds us up and is our refuge (Isaiah 49:8–11, Exodus 11:4, Deuteronomy 1:31, Deuteronomy 32:27, Psalm 18:35, Psalm 37:17, Psalm 41:12, Isaiah 41:10, Isaiah 46:4, Psalm 31:23, Psalm 37:28, Psalm 146:9, Proverbs 2:8, Isaiah 49:8, 2 Timothy 4:18, Psalm 28:7, Psalm 40:17)

God wants all to be saved (2 Peter 3:9, 1 Peter 3:18–20)

Cannot mix evil with love (Lamentations 3:38)

Love covers a multitude of sins (Proverbs 10:12, Hosea 6:6, Matthew 9:13)

Angels

Angels are servants (Matthew 4:11, Matthew 18:10–14, Hebrews 1:13–14)

We have guardian angels (Matthew 18:10)

Fallen angels (2 Peter 2:1–5, Revelation 7, Revelation 12:4)

Angels that sinned (Jude 6, 2 Peter 2:4)

Do not worship angels (Revelation 19:10–11)

Angels are servants (Hebrews 1:13–14)

Baptism

Moses baptized (1 Corinthians 10:1–6)

Why baptize (Romans 6:1–4)

Jesus was baptized (Matthew 3:16, Matthew 20:21–23)

Holy Spirit baptizes (Acts 1:5)

Jesus does not baptize (John 4:2)

What name to be baptized in (Acts 2:38, 1 Corinthians 12:13, Galatians 3:27)

LOVE IS

Salvation

> Believing God is salvation (Exodus 12)
> Moses believed God; it was accounted to him as righteousness (Hebrews 11:23–29)
> The law upon salvation is fulfilled (Romans chapters 3–8)
> Jesus is our Passover (Exodus 12, 1 Corinthians 5:7, John 1:29, John 1:36, Acts 8:32, 1 Peter 1:19, Revelation 5:6–13, Revelation 6:1, Revelation 6:16)
>
> God buried Moses (Deuteronomy 34:1–6)
> The law is our schoolmaster (Galatians 5:1–18)
> Salvation is to know God (John 17:4)
> True church is a completely new covenant (Matthew 9:14–17)
> The blood of Jesus washes away our sins (1 John 1:7–10, 1 John 2:1–3)
> After being saved, we are at peace with God (Romans 5:1–11)
> Man has not enough strength to live a sinless life (Romans 7:19–21)
> Jesus replaced the old covenant with the new (Hebrews 10:1–9, Hebrews chapters 8–9)
> Burned offerings were never intended to save men (Psalm 40, Hebrews 10:7–39)
> Sin is forgiven (1 John 5:16, 1 John 1:8–10)
> Jesus is the only way to salvation (John 3:16, John 6:26–35, John 7:37–38, John 10:1–18)
> We are baptized into the Holy Spirit (1 Corinthians 12:13)
> God is our shield and our everlasting great reward (Genesis 15:1)
> Jesus came preaching peace (Ephesians 2:15–17)

Why should man learn about God?

> 1) God is our closest relative; he is our Father.
> 2) We are the heirs of salvation (Hebrews 1:13–14).

3) God has the answers to man's most important questions: Who am I? How did I get here? Where am I going?
4) Jesus bought us with his blood; he is our Lord.
5) One day each of us will stand before God.
6) God is love, and he loves each of us.
7) There is an adversary who wishes to destroy each of us.

Not everyone will enter heaven (Matthew 7:21).

Salvation

The righteousness of Jesus keeps the saved

> Our righteousness cannot save us (Ezekiel 33:13, Isaiah 64:5–6, Genesis 15:6, Genesis 28:15, Psalm 34:20, Psalm 121:4, John 17:11, Philippians 4:7, 2 Thessalonians 3:3, 2 Timothy 1:12, 1 Peter 1:5, Jude 24, Revelation 3:10, 2 Peter 1:1, Joshua 24:17, Deuteronomy 6:24, 2 Samuel 8:6, Nehemiah 9:6, Psalm 31:23, Psalm 37:28, Psalm 146:9, Proverbs 2:8, Isaiah 49:8, 2 Timothy 4:18, 2 Chronicles 16:9, Psalm 91:4, Luke 21:18, Job 11:18, Psalm 91:5, Psalm 112:5, Psalm 125:1, Proverbs 1:33)
> God protects his children (Ezekiel 33:22, Deuteronomy 32:11, Psalm 57:1, Psalm 63:7, Psalm 91:1, Psalm 121:5, Song of Solomon 2:3, Isaiah 25:4, Isaiah 32:2, Isaiah 51:16, Matthew 23:37, Psalm 34:7, Psalm 41:2, Psalm 91:4, Genesis 35:5, Exodus 14:20, 2 Kings 6:17, Ezra 8:31, Daniel 6:22, Revelation 7:3, Genesis 26:24, Numbers 21:34, Jude 6:23, 1 Kings 17:13, 2 Kings 6:16, Isaiah 41:10, Isaiah 43:1–3, Matthew 10:30–31, Matthew 28:5, Luke 12:32, Revelation 1:17–18, Psalm 91:10, Psalm 112:8, Proverbs 1:33, Proverbs 3:23, Proverbs 12:21, Proverbs 21:31, Isaiah 32:18, Jeremiah 23:6, Genesis 15:1)
> Man is saved and kept for Jesus's name's sake (1 John 2:12)
> God did not destroy Israel for God's name's sake (Ezekiel 20:7–10, Ezekiel 18:22, Numbers 14:11–24, Isaiah 43:25)

The law has no dominion over the saved (Romans 7:1–4)

All the law is fulfilled in one word: *love* (Genesis 5:14, 1 Timothy 1:5, 1 Peter 1:22, John 8:42, Proverbs 10:12)

The law cannot save man (John 8:1–12, Ephesians 2:15, Colossians 2:14, Hebrews 7:18, Hebrews 8:13, Hebrews 10:1, Hebrews 12:27, Hebrews 12:27, Romans 3:20)

Upon salvation, it's an immediate event, there is no trial period, you are saved forever (Romans 7:18–25, Matthew 26:30–46)

The saved know Jesus and the Father (1 John 2:29, John 1:12–16, John 10:7–18, John 14:23, John 15:15, John 17:1)

The saved are God's sons (John 1:12, Romans 8:14, Job 38, John 10:34, Psalm 82:6, Ezekiel 18:4)

Man has two bodies (Matthew 10:28, Luke 16, Luke 20:37, Ecclesiastes 12)

The Word of God

God's Word is the standard used to test for truth (Numbers 5:23)

God told kings of Israel to make copies of God's Word (Deuteronomy 17:18, Joshua 8:30–35)

God told kings of Israel to read God's Word (Deuteronomy 17:18, Joshua 1:8, Joshua 23:6, 2 Kings 23:2)

God holds man accountable to know and do God's Word (Deuteronomy 74:1–14, Mark 12:26)

Example of God's Word being read to kings and people (Exodus 24:7, Deuteronomy 30:11–14)

Jesus read God's Word to the people (Luke 4:16–30)

Paul taught we must read the Word of God (Colossians 4:16)

God's Word is used to verify events (Luke 3:1–6, Acts 1:20–26)

God's Word is used to verify the identity of Jesus (Luke 20:27–44, John 20:30–31)

We are responsible to teach our children God's Word (John 8:34–35)

Result of teachers not teaching the Word of God (Isaiah 29)

Truth will set you free (2 Thessalonians 2:10–12)
God wants truth (Psalm 51:1–6)
Jesus said, "Do not be deceived" (Matthew 24)
Must grow in God's statutes and know them (Leviticus 26:1–13)

Ark of the Covenant

> Example of David not knowing how to move the Ark of the Covenant (1 Chronicles 13)
> Example after David learned how to move the Ark of the Covenant (1 Chronicles 15)
> How to move the Ark of the Covenant (Numbers 7:1–9)

We must know God (1 John 3:2, 1 John 3:14, 1 John 3:24, John 7:3)

God is full of wisdom, knowledge, and understanding (1 Samuel 2:3, Isaiah 40:28, Daniel 2:22, 1 Corinthians 3:20, 1 John 3:20, Psalm 69:5, Psalm 139:2–4, Jeremiah 10:1–12, Daniel 2:20, Romans 11:33, Romans 16:27, 1 Corinthians 1:25)

God knows our thoughts (Proverbs 15:11, Jeremiah 20:12, Matthew 12:25, Matthew 22:18, Mark 2:8, Luke 6:8, Luke 11:17, Luke 16:15, John 2:25, Acts 15:8)

God knows everything about us (Psalm 1:6, Psalm 119:168, Psalm 139:3, Proverbs 5:21, Jeremiah 16:17, Jeremiah 32:19, Nahum 1:7, John 1:48, John 10:3, John 10:14, 1 Corinthians 8:3, Galatians 4:9, 2 Timothy 2:19)

If you have seen Jesus, you have seen the Father (John 9)

God's ways are mysteries to man.

> The great day of God's wrath (Revelation 6:16–17)

God's Will

> What is God's will (2 Peter 3:9, 1 Thessalonians 5:9–18, John 6:38–40, John 9:31)

God does everything according to God's own will (Ephesians 1:11)
The complete Bible was written by the will of God (2 Peter 1:21)
Only the will of God can save you (Romans 2:17–29)
The elect are predestinated by the will of God (Ephesians 1:5)
Jesus came to do the will of God (John 4:34, John 6:38–40, Galatians 1:4, Hebrews 10:7–10)
God's will was that Jesus would finish God's work (John 5:34–47)
Jesus made known the mysteries of God's will (Ephesians 1:9)
Examples of the will of Jesus (Luke 5:12–13, John 5:21, John 21:20–23)
We are to be filled with the knowledge of God's will (Colossians 1:9, Colossians 4:12)
Christians can do only what God allows them to do (1 Thessalonians 2:1–4)
Apostle John taught to do God's will (1 John 2:17, Revelation 17:17)
Paul taught by example to do God's will (1 Thessalonians 3:1–11, Ephesians 1:1, Romans 1:10, Romans 15:32, 1 Corinthians 1:1)
Paul taught directly to do God's will (1 Thessalonians 4:1–4, Ephesians 5:17, Romans 9:15–19, Romans 12:1–3)
Blind man that Jesus healed taught to do God's will (John 9:31)
Jesus taught that we must do God's will (Matthew 7:21, John 7:17)
Jesus taught that we are not God's children unless we do God's will (Matthew 12:50, Mark 3:35)
Jesus taught the last generation they must do God's will (Luke 12:47)
The beloved Apostle John taught to pray in God's will (1 John 5:14)
Jesus taught by example to pray in God's will (Matthew 26:39, Mark 14:36, Luke 22:42)
Jesus directly taught to pray in the will of God (Luke 11:2)

The Holy Spirit prays for us in God's will (Romans 8)
Jesus is the only way to salvation (John 3:16–18, John 6:26–35, John 7:37–38, John 10:1–18)
Must know God to be saved (Hosea 4:1–6)

God's rest (Hebrews 4:1)
We are to wait on the return of the Lord (at the end of this war)
We are to enter into the rest of our God and wait upon him (Genesis 2:1–3, Hebrews 4:1–11, Isaiah 40:28–31, Psalm 27)
We are to wait upon the Lord, trusting in him, believing in him, and accept the work done by him and his Son, Jesus Christ (Hebrews 11:23–29, Psalm 40:1–6, Psalm 62:1–2, Isaiah 28:1–12)

Jesus is our Passover Lamb (Exodus 12, 1 Corinthians 5:7, John 3:16–18)
God is our shelter that protects us from the evils of this world (Psalm 61:1–4, Proverbs 19:23)
Jesus writes (engraves) his truth in our hearts. This is part of God's covenant with us (Hebrews 10:1–16)

God hates lies (Proverbs 6:16–19)
Satan is the father of lies (John 8:44, John 8:55)
Drunkards will not inherit the kingdom of God (1 Corinthians 9:12)

If we trust in the Lord, he will come and rescue us (Psalm 40:7–10)
After being saved, we still cry out to the Lord for his mercy and grace (Psalm 40:11)
We cry out because of the evil world we live in and because we still sin; sin threatens our love and joy for our Father (Psalm 40:12)
It is the pleasure of the Lord to save man (Psalm 40:13)
Happy is the man who trusts in the Lord (Psalm 40:4)

Too many to number are the wonderful, mighty works of God (Psalm 40:5)
God's thoughts toward us are too many to number (Psalm 40:5)
The Lord gave David a joy so great he could only praise God (Psalm 40:3)
David waited patiently for the Lord; the Lord inclined his ear unto David and heard his cry (Psalm 40:1)
It is a mystery how we, as a believer, become the temple of the Holy Spirit (Colossians 1:27)
Wait on the Lord (Lamentations 3:26, Isaiah 64:4, Isaiah 40:28–31, Psalm 27)
The elect will be priests during the thousand-year reign (Revelation 20:6)
What eternity is like (Isaiah 65)
Women not to teach (1 Timothy 2:9–15, 1 Timothy 5)
God teaches his own (Matthew 5:1–2)
What Jesus taught (Matthew 5:1–48)
Purpose of parables (Matthew 13:10–11)
The true church is a completely new covenant (Matthew 9:14–17)
God wants our love, not sacrifice (Hosea 6:6, Matthew 9:10–13)
Love not the world (1 John 2:15–17)
The blood of Jesus washes away our sins (1 John 1:7–10)
Our sins are forgiven for Jesus's name's sake (1 John 2:12)
The gospel is spread by believers and is the power of God to save (Romans 1:16–17, John 17:20)
The anger of God toward those who suppress the truth (Romans 1:18)
The unsaved willingly suppress the truth (Romans 1:19–23)

The work of the Holy Spirit (John 5:32)
By judging others, you put condemnation on yourself (Luke 6:37, Romans 2:1–5, Matthew 7:1–5)
Sent as sheep among wolves (Luke 10:3)
Required to produce fruit (2 Peter 1:5–8)
The Holy Spirit testifies to you of the truth (1 John 5:10)

The armor of God (Ephesians 6:10–19)
Live for God in the Spirit (1 Peter 4:6)
At death, man returns to God (Luke 23:46, Ecclesiastes 12:6–7, John 3:13, Luke 20:27–44)
After being saved, we are at peace with God (Romans 5:1–11)
If we believe a lie, God must allow us to believe that lie (Romans 11:1–11, 2 Corinthians 4:1–4, 2 Thessalonians 2:11)

The work of God (John 6:24–71)
Salvation is to know God (John 17:1–4)
Feed others the meat of the Word (Hebrews 6)
We are to learn from nature (Romans 1:26)
How God heals the sick (James 5)
When Jesus opens a door, no man can shut it (Revelation 3:7–13)
How to dwell with God (Exodus 29)
Jesus gave us the keys to heaven (Matthew 15:17–19)
God will not put upon you more than you can bear (1 Corinthians 10:13)
What the church should teach today (Revelation 2:9, Revelation 3:9, 1 Corinthians 13)
The secret that has been kept secret since the foundation of the world concerning the fall of Satan (Matthew 13:35)
Know the mystery of God's will (Deuteronomy 29:1–4)
The Holy Spirit brings all things to our remembrance (John 14)
We have authority over Satan (Luke 10:19, Isaiah 54:17)
We are trees (Isaiah 61:2–4, Romans 11:1–24), olive tree (Hosea 14:1–10)
The elect will not worship anti-Christ (Romans 11:1–4, 1 Kings 19:18)

God is the father of Jesus

For sin shall not have dominion over you (Romans 6:14)
Love your enemies (Matthew 5:43–44)

Jesus is coming back to receive his bride, the church (1 Corinthians 12:13)
The elect receive their assignment and the Holy Spirit before their birth (Luke 1:1–45)
God corrects the ones he loves (Proverbs 3:12–13)
Train up a child in the way he should go, and when he is old, he will not depart from it (Proverbs 22:6)

Church plants seeds of truth (Romans 1:16–17)
What happens to the church (Luke 9:28–36)
Jesus taught who is greatest in the church (Luke 9:46–50)
The church is in Jesus (Luke 10:16–20)
Jesus taught the church how to pray (Luke 11:1–13)
Why Jesus lives in the church (Luke 11:14–36, Hosea 6:1–11, Hosea 14:1–9, Isaiah 7:14, Isaiah 9:6–7, Isaiah 11:1–3, Isaiah 6:1, Isaiah 50:6, Isaiah 53:1–12, Isaiah 12:1–6, Isaiah 14:1–32, Isaiah 28:16)

Love of our father is shown in his grace (Jonah 3:10, Jonah 4:11)
Paul fought the good fight and lets us know we are to fight the good fight as well (2 Timothy 4:1–7)
A woman is not to rule over a man (Isaiah 3:1–26, Genesis 3:16, Revelation 16)
What we are to teach (Titus 2:15)

God's forgiveness of sin

Transgression: revolt (national, moral, or religious), rebellion, sin, trespass

God declares he will forgive revolt and sin (Exodus 34:7, Exodus 20:5)
The sin offering of Jesus's blood was for the revolt in their sins (Leviticus 16:16–21)

The Lord is long-suffering and of great mercy, forgiving iniquity and revolt (Numbers 14:18)
David said the transgressors rebelled against God (Psalm 5:10)
David prayed to be innocent of the great revolt (Psalm 19:13, Psalm 25:7, Psalm 32:1, Psalm 32:5)
David said the transgressions of the wicked reveal they don't fear God and they lie (Psalm 36:1–4)
David acknowledged his transgressions in prayer (Psalm 51:1–19)
David said God will purge our revolt away (Psalm 65:3)
God removes the sins from the true church as far as the east is from the west (Psalm 103:12)
The wicked is trapped by the rebellion that comes out of his mouth (Proverbs 12:13)
God forgiving sins is his glory (Proverbs 19:11)

Why man must know the truth (Deuteronomy 4:1–14)
The truth will set you free
Good outweighing the bad will not get you to heaven
Not knowing the truth hides God's mercy and grace
The price Jesus paid was so great it would be an insult not to know the truth
The lies cause man to look at God as his enemy
Satan killed Jesus; because of this, God is righteous to punish Satan

Why the truth is important (Ezekiel 3:16–21, Psalm 22:23, Isaiah 42:12, Isaiah 52:1–21, Luke 2:13–14, John 15:8, Romans 15:6, 1 Corinthians 6:20, 2 Corinthians 4:6, Romans 1:16, 2 Thessalonians 1:12, Revelation 5:11–12, Revelation 7:11–12, Revelation 11:17, Revelation 14:13, Revelation 19:5)

Pastors at end-time (Jeremiah 28, Jeremiah 23, Micah chapters 1–3, Jeremiah 26)

LOVE IS

The great responsibility of teachers of God's Word (Ezekiel 3:16–21, Ezekiel 4:1–17, Ezekiel 5:1–4, Ezekiel 8, Ezekiel 9:6)

What God says true fasting is (Isaiah 58:6–8)
Deception at the end (Matthew 24)
Condition of the church (Jeremiah 5, Ezekiel 13, Ezekiel 11:1–25)
The unsaved willingly suppress the truth (Romans 1:19–23)
Deceptions of the Rapture (Ezekiel 13:1)
Man does not tell the truth about God (Isaiah 48:1–22)
You must teach the truth about God's Word (John 8, Ezekiel 6:1–14, Ezekiel 7:20–27, Isaiah 59:1–21, Ezekiel 8, 1 Timothy 4, Ezekiel 13, Ezekiel 11:1–25, Jeremiah 18:188)
Sons do not pay for sins of their fathers (Ezekiel 18:1–23)
The ten virgins who did not have enough oil (Matthew 25:1–13)

What is a lie? (Proverbs 30:5–6, 1 John 2:4, 1 John 2:21, 1 John 2:27, 2 John 1–11)
What is the truth? God loves his children (Psalm 40:1–11, Psalm 58:1–3, Acts 26:1–25, Colossians 1:5–6, 1 Thessalonians 2:13, 2 Thessalonians 2:10–13, 1 John 5:6, John 3:16)
The law is truth (Malachi 2:6)
God is truth (Psalm 31:5, Psalm 33:4, Psalm 57:9–10, Psalm 86:11, Psalm 89:14, Psalm 89:49, Isaiah 10:20, Isaiah 15:5, Isaiah 25:1, Isaiah 65:16, John 1:14, John 3:21, John 7:37–40, Jeremiah 4:2, John 8:30–32, John 8:40, John 8:44, John 15:26, John 16:7, John 16:13, Daniel 4:37, Daniel 10:21, John 17:17–19, Romans 3:4, Romans 15:8, 3 John 1:1–12, Hebrews 6:18, Matthew 22:16, Titus 1:2, Deuteronomy 32:4, 2 Samuel 7:28, Psalm 146:6, Mark 12:14)

Truth will make you free (1 Timothy 4:1–4, John 8:32–44, John 14:6)
Truth is wisdom (Proverbs 8:7)

God's truth will last forever (Psalm 117:2, Psalm 146:6, Proverbs 12)

Truth is the power that saves lives (Genesis 2:15–17, Genesis 42:16, Psalm 15:1–2, Psalm 25:5, Psalm 26:3, Psalm 40:11, Psalm 43:3, Psalm 61:7, Psalm 69:12–14, Psalm 85:10, Psalm 91:4, Psalm 108:4, Proverbs 3:1–4, Proverbs 3:12, Proverbs 17:22, Daniel 7:15–19, Mark 5:33–34, James 1:18, 1 Peter 1:22)

God cannot lie (1 Samuel 15:29, Psalm 89:34–36, Psalm 25:10, Psalm 132:11, Habakkuk 2:3, Hebrews 6:18, Titus 1:2–10, Exodus 34:4–6)

If you are reading this book and would like to become a Christian, that is the best decision you have made in your life. All you have to do is say this simple prayer: "Dear Lord, I believe you died for me, rose again, and are in heaven right now. Come into my heart. Come into my life and do something with it. I will serve you for the rest of my life. Amen."

If you said that prayer, you are now a child of the living God. He will never leave you or forsake you. Jesus paid a heavy price for us. He loves us more than we will ever know. Talk to him, which is prayer. Whatever you need, the Lord is quite willing and able to help you. God bless you.

Jesus prospers through and because of truth (Psalm 45:4)

God hates lies (Proverbs 6:16–19)

God cannot lie (1 Samuel 15:29, Psalm 89:34–36, Psalm 25:10, Psalm 132:11, Habakkuk 2:3, Hebrews 6:18, Titus 1:2–10, Exodus 34:4–6)

Truth is what God gives his people (Genesis 24:27, Genesis 32:9–11, 1 Kings 17:24, Zechariah 8:3, Psalm 57:3, Psalm 100:5, Proverbs 14:22, Micah 7:20, John 8:40–46, 2 Peter 1:12, 1 John 1:6–8, 1 John 2:4, 1 John 2:21, 1 John 2:27, 1 John 4:6, 1 John 5:6, 2 John 1:1–4, 3 John 1:1–12)

Truth is the only way man can worship God (Joshua 24:14, Judges 9:15, 1 Samuel 12:24, 1 Kings 2:1–4, 1 Kings 3:1–6,

2 Kings 20:3, 2 Kings 20:19, Psalm 26:3, Psalm 54:5, Psalm 145:18, Isaiah 61:8, Zechariah 8:8, Zechariah 8:16, John 4:22–24, 1 John 18:24)

God's children are to speak truth (Proverbs 12:19, Zephaniah 3:13, Zechariah 8:16, Malachi 2:6, 2 Corinthians 12:6, Ephesians 4:25, Ephesians 6:14, Exodus 18:21, Psalm 40:4, Proverbs 14:1–8, Isaiah 63:7–10, Colossians 3:1–10, Ephesians 4:14–15, 2 Corinthians 11:31, James 3:14, 1 Timothy 2:7, 1 John 2:27, Zephaniah 3:13)

Warning against falsehood (Leviticus 19:11, Psalm 5:6, Psalm 31:18, Psalm 101:7, Psalm 120:2, Proverbs 12:22, Proverbs 19:9, Proverbs 21:6, Colossians 3:9, Revelation 21:8)

The purpose of God's children is to declare God's truth (Psalm 30:1–12, Psalm 40:10, Psalm 45:17, Psalm 51:6, Psalm 60:3–4, Psalm 71:22, Psalm 85:11, Psalm 115:1, Proverbs 22:21, Daniel 10:21, Daniel 11:2, Hosea 4:1, Zechariah 8:16, Zechariah 8:19, Malachi 2:1–7, Ecclesiastes 12:10, Isaiah 38:17–19, Isaiah 48:1, Jeremiah 5:1–4, Jeremiah 33:1–9, Matthew 22:16, John 8:30–32, Acts 26:25, Romans 15:8)

Live for God in the Spirit (1 Peter 4:6)
After being saved, we are at peace with God (Romans 5:1–11)
God corrects the one he loves (Proverbs 3:12–13)
Why God destroyed the first generation in the wilderness (Ezekiel 20)
In the day that Jesus comes (Isaiah 28:5)
Precept upon precept, line upon line, here a little, there a little (Isaiah 28:10)
Jesus is the foundation, the cornerstone (Isaiah 28:16)

To be a disciple of Jesus, you must love him more than anyone (Luke 14:26–27)
God is not the author of confusion (1 Corinthians 14:33)
Love covers a multitude of sins (Proverbs 10:12)
We are to love our enemies (Matthew 5:43–44)

God is love (1 John 4:16)
Rebellion hinders nourishment (Genesis 4:1–12)
God does not want our sacrifices; he wants our love (Hosea 6:6, Matthew 9:13)
Faith comes by God calling us; hearing God's call comes by reading God's Word (Romans 10:17)
Jesus is the Word (John 1:1–3, Revelation 19:11–13)
God is wisdom (Proverbs 8:22–30)
Why is God so concerned with man? (Jeremiah 4:19)
Abraham believed if he sacrificed his son, God would raise him from the dead (Hebrews 11:17–19, Genesis 15:6)
Jesus came to do the will of his Father (John 10:14–18)
Jesus freely gave his life (John 10:14–18)
All have sinned and come short of the glory of God (Romans 3:23, Romans 3:10)
God told Abraham he would send his perfect ram, Jesus (Genesis 22:15–18)
Jesus came through the seed of Abraham (Matthew 1:1)
Jesus is the only way (John 14:6, John 10:4)
Jesus has the key to heaven and the key to the gate of his enemies (Matthew 16:13–20, Revelation 1:18)

Jesus is the good shepherd; we are the sheep (John 10:14)
God wants all of us to be saved, no one left out! (2 Peter 3:9)
God will tell all men about his son, Jesus Christ (Colossians 1:1–6, Matthew 24:14)
All things exist by Jesus (Colossians 1:7–29)
There was a first earth age (Colossians 1:26, 1 Corinthians 2:7, Ephesians 1:4–5, 2 Peter 3:5–6)
Jesus saw Satan fall as lightning (Luke 10:17–18)
All of God's sons witnessed recreation (Job 38:3–7)
We cannot put a private interpretation on God's Word (2 Peter 1:20)
Jesus is the only begotten Son of God and Son of Man (John 1:18, John 3:16, 1 John 4:9, Luke 5:24, John 5:46–47)

Fallen angels were cast into chains of darkness (2 Peter 2:4, Revelation 20:1–5)

All souls are God's sons: God owns all souls (John 1:12, Romans 8:14, John 10:34, Psalm 82:6, Ezekiel 18:4)

Man has a flesh body and a spiritual body (Matthew 10:28, 1 Corinthians 15:35–58)

At death, our spiritual body, housing our soul, returns to God (Ecclesiastes 1:6–7, 2 Corinthians 5:6–8)

Angels are not God's sons; they are servants (Hebrews 1:13–14, Matthew 18:10)

Angels are our servants as well (Matthew 18:10–14, Hebrews 1:13–14)

Jesus is the beginning and the ending (Revelation 1:8)

Jesus is Emmanuel, God with us (Matthew 1:23)

The entire Bible was written about Jesus (Hebrews 10:7)

Jesus foretold us all things (Mark 13:23)

The will of God is for Jesus to raise all believers on the last day (John 6:38–40)

God knew us in the first earth age (Jeremiah 1:4–5, Romans 9:11–13, Ephesians 1:4–5)

God destroyed the first earth age (Jeremiah 4:23–26, Genesis 1:2, Hebrews 12:25–27, Hebrews 12:27, 2 Peter 3:5–6)

Water represents man (Genesis 1:2, Revelation 17:15, Revelation 20:13, Hebrews 12:1, Revelation 1:7)

Jesus is the Word; he is the Light, and he made all things, and without him was nothing made that was made (John 1:1–5, John 3:16–20, 2 Corinthians 4:6)

God is a consuming fire (Hebrews 12:27)

Jesus is the light (Genesis 1:3)

The light of the knowledge of the glory of God in the face of Jesus Christ (2 Corinthians 4:6)

Jesus went to the gulf preaching when he rose from the dead, and many were saved (1 Peter 3:18–20)

The earth's atmosphere represents the Holy Spirit, wind (Genesis 2:7, Ezekiel 37:9–14, Acts 1:1–8)

Jesus sent the Holy Spirit (John 16:1–7)

The purpose of the Holy Spirit is to glorify Jesus (John 16:13–15)

The Holy Spirit seals us in himself (Ephesians 4:30, 1 Corinthians 12:13)

Jesus is the divider (Matthew 25:31–34)

The gospel is the power to save (Romans 1:13–17, Luke 16:16)

In John 3:16, God tells us that God so loved the world that he gave his only begotten Son that whomever believes should not die but have everlasting life. He actually died for us. He let them torture him, spit on him, do their heart's desire to him. Whatever their hatred could come up with to show their disrespect, Jesus allowed without revenge entering his heart. There was nothing but love in the heart of Jesus. Can you imagine? Could you or I do the same? I think not! Oh, it's not that the possibility did not exist. The Son of Man side of Jesus may have made it possible to do something other than what he did, but the Son of God side could do nothing but the will of his Father God. Jesus is still calling every man to be saved and spend eternity with him. His heart weeps for those who choose not to live with him forever. He promises an abundant life, in fullest measure. I want that promise, don't you?

Does God not want his children to fear him? (Matthew 10:28–30, Proverbs 1:7)

God is not at war with or angry with man due to sin (Romans 5:6–8, Luke 5:27–32)

Man cannot achieve a state of righteousness (Romans 7:19–21, Matthew 26:30–46)

It is Jesus's righteousness that covers our sin (Romans 3:21–31, Romans 5:17–21, Romans 10:4, 1 Corinthians 1:30, Philippians 3:9)

God's children perish for lack of knowledge (Hosea 4:6)

God is faithful and just to forgive sins if we confess them to him (1 John 1:9)

All things were created for our Father's pleasure (Revelation 4:11)
God hated Esau because he sold his birthright for a bowl of food (Romans 9:10–13, Malachi 1:1–5)
The start of different races (Genesis 2:1)
There is nothing new under the sun (Ecclesiastes chapter 1)
We are to enter into God's rest (Isaiah 40:28–31, Psalm 27, Genesis 2:1–3, Hebrews 4:1–11)

God is a spirit and can only be worshipped in spirit (John 4:24)
Moses was chosen by God because he believed God (Hebrews 11:23–29)
Jesus is our Passover Lamb (Exodus 12, 1 Corinthians 5:7)
Joshua led God's people into the Promised Land (Joshua 1:1–2)
Jesus is the only way to heaven (John 3:16–18)
Moses died on Mount Nebo, God buried Moses (Deuteronomy 34:1–6)
Moses was one hundred and twenty years old when he died (Deuteronomy 34:7)
Freedom from bondage is a gift from our Lord and Savior Jesus Christ.
Blood is required to be set free from bondage (Exodus 11, Exodus 12, Genesis 3:7, Genesis 3:21)
It brings God and Jesus great pleasure to provide man a new beginning (Revelation 4:11)
The river flowing through Eden represents man (Genesis 2:10–14)
Satan was perfect in all his ways until the sin of pride was found in him (Ezekiel 28:15)
Jesus was sent when the fullness of time had come (Galatians 4:4)
It brought great excitement to God to create and care for man; God loves us very much (Genesis 2:18–25, Revelation 4:11, John 3:16)
God loves us so much he supplies our needs before we know we have a need (Genesis 2:18, Matthew 6:8)

Man is appointed once to be born and once to die (Hebrews 9:27–28)

Jesus was sent before the foundation of the world (Genesis 1:3, 1 Corinthians 2:7, Romans 16:25–26, 1 Peter 1:19–20, Revelation 13:8)

The saved are the bride of Jesus (Ephesians 5)

Through the hardest times, Jesus would endure; his concerns were for us, not himself (Matthew 4:4, Luke 23:34)

Satan has been sentenced to death (Ezekiel 28:1–10, Revelation 20)

Man adds to our Father's Word (Genesis 2:7–25, Genesis 2:17, Matthew 15:1–20)

Satan is the father of lies.

What caused the fall of Satan? Pride (Ezekiel 28:11–19)

All have sinned and come short of the glory of God (Romans 3:9–12)

Sin opened the eyes of Adam and Eve to evil (Genesis 3:7)

Love is the fulfillment of all the law (Luke 10:27, Galatians 5:14)

The law is our schoolmaster, teaching man's need for Jesus (Galatians 3:24–25, Galatians 5:1–18)

Man is saved by the Holy Spirit calling us to Jesus Christ (Matthew 16:13–20)

The elect are born of God (1 John 2:29)

The teacher of God can only plant seeds and then depend upon God to make the seeds grow (Matthew 13:1–9, John 5:31–47, John 6:44–46, Matthew 16:13–17)

God never sleeps (Psalm 121, Isaiah 40:18–31)

God and Jesus are one (John 14:1–11, Matthew 1:23)

God corrects the ones he loves (Proverb 3:12–13)

The man rejecting our Father can repent and be welcomed by our Father back home (Luke 15:11–32 [the prodigal son])

Baptism

> Moses baptized (1 Corinthians 10:1–6)
> Why baptism (Romans 6:1–4)
> Jesus was baptized (Matthew 3:16, Matthew 20:21–23)
> The Holy Spirit baptizes (Acts 1:5)
> Jesus does not baptize (John 4:2)
> What name to be baptized in (Acts 2:38, Acts 8:12, 1 Corinthians 12:13, Galatians 3:27)
>
> Moses told Israel to stand still and see the salvation of God (Exodus 4:13)
> The Lord shall fight for you (Exodus 14:14)
> Rightly dividing the word of truth
>
> The birth of Jesus (Micah 5:2, Isaiah 7:14, Isaiah 6:1, Isaiah 9:6–7, Isaiah 11:1–3, Luke 1:28–38, Luke 2:6–14)
>
> Calvary, Jesus's death on the cross (Isaiah 50:6, Isaiah 53:1–12, Daniel 9:24–27, Zechariah 9:9, Zechariah 11:12–13)
>
> Day of Pentecost, descent of the Holy Spirit (Joel 2:25–32, Luke 24:39, Acts 4:31, John 16:7, John 16:13)
>
> Destruction of Jerusalem, Jews scattered, AD 70 (Matthew 24:1–2, Daniel 9:26, Matthew 24:1–2)
>
> Return of the Jews: May 14, 1948 (Ezekiel 20:40–44, Ezekiel 34:11–28, Ezekiel 36:24–32, Ezekiel 37:1–28, Jeremiah 3:18, Jeremiah 16:14–15, Jeremiah 23:3–8, Jeremiah 31:8, Isaiah 11:11–16, Isaiah 60:8–16, Amos 9:11–12, Hosea 3:4–5, Hosea 6:1–2)
>
> The Lord has spoken about bringing Israel's children back to their homeland—a prophecy in the book of Jeremiah (Jeremiah 16:14–21)

Israel (God's chosen people and God's chosen land), at Jesus's Second Coming, the land of Israel will be where Jesus's feet touch the earth. Israel, your Messiah longs for you.

Mysteries of the Gospel

>Mysteries of the kingdom of God (Mark 4:11)
>Blindness in part has happened to Israel, until the fullness of the Gentiles comes in (Romans 11:25)
>Of Jesus ordained before the world (1 Corinthians 2:7, John 17:5, John 17:24)
>Of the victory over death (1 Corinthians 15:51)
>Of God's will (Ephesians 1:9, Deuteronomy 29:1–4)
>Of God's wisdom, salvation of the Gentiles (Ephesians 3:3, Ephesians 3:4, Ephesians 3:9)
>Of the church being the body of Jesus (Ephesians 5:32)
>Of the Gospel (Ephesians 6:19)
>Of Jesus in the church, the hope of glory (Colossians 1:26, Colossians 1:27)
>Of Jesus (Colossians 2:2)
>Of iniquity (2 Thessalonians 2:7)
>Of the faith (1 Timothy 3:9)
>Of godliness (1 Timothy 3:16)
>Of seven stars (Revelation 1:20)
>Declared to the servants and prophets finished (Revelation 10:7)
>Of Babylon (Revelation 17:5)
>Of the woman on the beast (Revelation 17:7)
>Anti-Christ in the last times (1 John 2:18)
>Instruction to all of God's children (1 Thessalonians 5:16–28)

More Mysteries

>Why the wicked prosper (Jeremiah 12:1)
>Being born of the Spirit (John 3:8)
>Knowledge and wisdom of God (Romans 11:33)

Our future life (1 Corinthians 15:51)
Christ and the church (Ephesians 5:29–33)
Jesus born in the flesh (1 Timothy 3:16)
Mystery of Christ (Colossians 4:3)
The work of God (Ecclesiastes 3:11, Ecclesiastes 8:17)
God's understanding (Isaiah 40:28, Romans 11:34–36, 1 Corinthians 2:16)
Work of Jesus (John 21:25)
God being unseen (Psalm 10:1, Psalm 13:1, Psalm 89:46, Isaiah 45:15, Deuteronomy 31:18, Psalm 44:24, Isaiah 1:15–20, Isaiah 59:2–19, Isaiah 64:7, Ezekiel 39:23–29, Micah 3:4)
The future (Proverbs 27:1, Ecclesiastes 3:22, Ecclesiastes 6:12, Ecclesiastes 8:7, Ecclesiastes 9:12, Ecclesiastes 10:14, Ecclesiastes 11:2, Matthew 24:43, Acts 20:22, James 4:14)

Study to show thyself approved (2 Timothy 2:15)
Shun profane and vain babblings (2 Timothy 2:16)
The feast, holy days of Israel (Leviticus chapter 23)
The parable of the faithful and wise steward (Luke 12:42–48)
The parable of the lost coin (Luke 15:8–10)
The parable of the prodigal son (Luke 15:11–32).
The rich man and Lazarus (Luke 16:19–31)
The unprofitable servant (Luke 7:10)

Candle under a bushel (Matthew 5:14–16, Mark 4:21–22, Luke 11:33–36)
Wise man builds on a rock (Matthew 7:24–27, Luke 6:47–49)
New doth on an old garment (Matthew 9:16, Mark 2:21, Luke 5:36)
New wine in an old bottle (Matthew 9:17, Mark 2:22, Luke 5:37–38)
The sower (Matthew 13:3–23, Mark 4:2–20, Luke 8:4–15)
The wheat and tares (Matthew 13:24–30)
The mustard seed (Matthew 13:31–32, Mark 4:30–32, Luke 13:18–19)
The leaven (Matthew 13:33, Luke 13:20–21)

The hidden treasure (Matthew 13:44)
The pearl of great price (Matthew 13:45–46)
The net (Matthew 13:47–50)
The lost sheep (Matthew 18:12–14, Luke 15:3–7)
The unforgiving servant (Matthew 18:23–35)
The laborers in the vineyard (Matthew 20:1–16)
The two sons (Matthew 21:28–32)
The wicked husbandman (Matthew 21:33–45, Mark 12:1–12, Luke 20:9–19)
The wedding feast (Matthew 22:2–14)
The fig tree (Matthew 24:32–44, Mark 15:28–32, Luke 21:28–33)
The wise and foolish virgins (Matthew 25:1–13)
The talents (Matthew 25:14–30)
The end-time tribulation will be shortened for the sake of the elect (Matthew 24:22)
When Jesus returns, he will gather to himself his elect (Matthew 24:31)

There are different forms of presenting information to others. Although I am happy with the form I have chosen up to this point, I think a different style would benefit the readers of this book. For those of you who would like a style that requires no research on your part, I present to you an easier form.

The main objective of me writing this book is to let you see how Jesus Christ in my life answers every question I've had. Whatever has come up in my life, when I pick up the Bible, I can be certain I will find the answer in the Scriptures.

So many times I have struggled to find what to do as I forge my way through life. Then I became a Christian. Although I may not always find an easy road to travel, I do find the Bible has the right road to navigate toward living the best life for myself and my family.

I have found in the center of everything is Jesus Christ. His love for us makes it easy for me to trust the advice I receive from his Word. Considering Jesus came to earth strictly for the purpose of going to the cross for you and me makes it easy to trust his rightful place in my life.

How many people do you know that would go to such extremes to protect you from death and hell? I know one; his name is Jesus Christ.

He wants to give to you an abundant life, in fullest measure. As has become evident to me, I am quite certain the purpose of Jesus does not revolve around himself. The Scriptures tell us that he is ever interceding for us, praying to our Father on our behalf. He is first class and will give to us a first-class life if we only give him the chance.

> That thou shouldest enter into covenant with the Lord thy God and into his oath which the Lord thy God maketh with thee this day.
>
> That he may establish thee today for a people unto himself, and that he may be unto thee a God, as he hath said unto thee, and as he hath sworn unto thy fathers, to Abraham, to Isaac, and to Jacob.
>
> Neither with you only do I make this covenant and this oath;
>
> But with him that standeth here with us this day before the Lord our God, and also with him that is not here with us this day. (Deuteronomy 29:12–15)

> Those that be planted in the House of the Lord shall flourish in the courts of our God.
>
> They shall still bring forth fruit in old age; they shall be fat and flourishing. (Psalm 92:13–14)

Every word you say will come to pass if you are full of righteousness in the anointing. Spiritual maturity lines up with decisions made on the Word of God. This has nothing to do with the length of time being saved.

> I give unto you power to tread on serpents and scorpions, and over all power of the enemy; and nothing shall by any means hurt you. (Luke 10:19)

Power has a name. That name is Jesus Christ.

We are anointed to win every time. God gives the ability to do whatever he wants us to do. When he positions us to do the work that he has called us to do, he gives us the ability to do whatever that may be.

Restoration comes when the anointing comes. He will restore unto us what the enemy has stolen from us. You are anointed. You are what God says you are. You have what God says you have. The anointing grows as righteousness grows.

The anointing is for service or mission. The anointing destroys yokes. The anointing will cause success while removing burdens. No burden can defeat the anointing. The anointing removes depression. Yield to the anointing and line up your thinking with the anointing. And it shall come to pass that burdens shall be removed from off your shoulders and yokes from off your neck.

Jesus as Portrayed by the Prophets

Pre-exile—Israel
Jonah—our resurrection and life
Amos—our heavenly husband
Hosea—healer of the backslider

Pre-exile—Judah
Obadiah—our Savior
Joel—our Restorer
Isaiah—our Messiah
Micah—our witness against rebellious nations
Nahum—our stronghold in the day of trouble
Habakkuk—our God of salvation
Zephaniah—our jealous Lord
Jeremiah—our righteous branch
Lamentations—our righteous branch

Exile—Israel and Judah together
Ezekiel—the Son of Man
Daniel—our smiting stone

Post-exile
Haggai—desire of all nations
Zechariah—the righteous branch
Malachi—the Son of righteousness
Revelation—our triumphant King

Names and titles applied to Jesus
Adam (1 Corinthians 15:45)

Advocate (1 John 2:1)
Almighty (Revelation 1:8)
Amen (Revelation 3:14)
Apostle of our faith (Hebrews 3:1)
Arm of the Lord (Isaiah 53:1)
Author and finisher of our faith (Hebrews 12:2)
Author of our salvation (Hebrews 5:9)

Beginning of the creation of God (Revelation 3:14, John 1:1–5)
Beloved Son (Matthew 12:18)
Blessed and only potentate, one who possesses great power (1 Timothy 6:15)
Branch (Isaiah 4:2, Isaiah 11:1, Jeremiah 21:5, Jeremiah 23:5, Jeremiah 33:15, Zechariah 3:8, Zechariah 6:12)
Bread of Life (John 6:32–35)

Captain of our salvation (Hebrews 2:10)
Chief Shepherd (1 Peter 5:4)
Christ of God—Christ = anointed (Luke 9:20)
Consolation of Israel (Luke 2:25)
Cornerstone (Psalm 118:22, Matthew 21:42, Acts 4:11, Ephesians 2:20, 1 Peter 2:6)
Counselor (Isaiah 9:6)
Creator (John 1:3)

Dayspring (Luke 1:78)
Daystar (2 Peter 1:19)
Deliverer (Romans 11:26)
Desired of all nations (Haggai 2:7)
Divider (Matthew 10:34–37)
Door (John 10:7)

Eagle (Exodus 19:4, Deuteronomy 32:11–12)
Elect of God (Isaiah 42:1)
Everlasting Father (Isaiah 9:6)
Eternal King of David's throne (Isaiah 9:6)

LOVE IS

Faithful witness (Revelation 1:5)
First and last (Revelation 1:17)
First begotten (Revelation 1:5)
Forerunner (Hebrews 6:20)

Glory of the Lord (Isaiah 40:5)
God (Isaiah 40:3, John 20:28)
God blessed (Romans 9:5)
Good Shepherd (John 10:11)
Governor (Matthew 2:6)
Great High Priest (Hebrews 4:14)

Head of the church (Ephesians 1:22)
Heir of all things (Hebrews 1:2)
Holy Child (Acts 4:27)
Holy One (Acts 3:14)
Holy One of God (Mark 1:24)
Holy One of Israel (Isaiah 41:14)
Horn of Salvation (Luke 1:69)

I am (John 8:58)
Image of God (2 Corinthians 4:4)
Immanuel—God is with us (Isaiah 7:14)

Jehovah's Anointed One (Psalm 2:2)
Jehovah—God is eternal (Isaiah 26:4)
Jesus—Savior of his people (Matthew 1:21)
Jesus of Nazareth (Matthew 21:11)
Judge of Israel (Micah 5:1)
Just One (Acts 7:52)
Jehovah, our righteousness (Jeremiah 23:5–6)

King (Zechariah 9:9)
King of the ages (1 Timothy 1:17)
King of the Jews (Matthew 2:2)
King of kings (1 Timothy 6:15)

King of saints—to the Jews first (2 Chronicles 6:41, Psalm 16:3, Psalm 106:16, 1 Peter 2:5), now to all believers (Acts 9:13, 1 Corinthians 16:1, 2 Corinthians 16:1, 2 Corinthians 1:1, 1 Corinthians 1:2)
Called out of the world to be God's people (Ephesians 4:1, Colossians 1:10)

Lawgiver (Isaiah 33:22)
Lamb (Revelation 13:8)
Lamb of God (John 1:29)
Leader (Isaiah 55:4)
Life (John 14:6)
Light (Isaiah 9:2, Isaiah 42:6, Matthew 4:16, Luke 1:79, John 1:4–9, John 8:12, John 12:35, John 35:46, 2 Corinthians 4:6, 1 John 2:8–10, Revelation 21:23, Psalm 27:1, Psalm 36:9, Psalm 84:11, Psalm 118:27, Isaiah 60:20, Micah 7:8, Habakkuk 3:4, 1 John 1:5, Revelation 22:5, Job 22:28, Psalm 97:11, Psalm 112:4, Proverbs 4:18, Isaiah 58:8, Isaiah 60:20, 2 Corinthians 5:13–14, John 9:4, Romans 13:12, Ephesians 5:8, Philippians 2:15, 1 Thessalonians 5:5–6, Luke 16:8)

Lion of the tribe of Judah (Revelation 5:5)
Lord of all (Acts 10:36)
Lord of glory (1 Corinthians 2:8)
Lord of lords (1 Timothy 6:15)
Lord of righteousness (Jeremiah 23:6)
Lord of the Sabbath (Luke 6:5)

Man of sorrow (Isaiah 53:3)
Master (Luke 15:5, Luke 8:24, Luke 8:45, Luke 9:33, Luke 9:49, Luke 17:13)
Mediator (1 Timothy 2:5)
Messenger (Matthew 21:37, John 6:38, John 7:29, John 8:42, John 9:4, John 10:36, John 17:8, John 17:21)
Messenger of the Covenant (Malachi 3:1)

Messiah—Hebrew for Christ, Christ = Anointed (Matthew 11:3, Matthew 16:16, Matthew 26:63, Luke 2:11, Luke 2:16, Luke 4:41, Luke 24:26, John 1:41, John 4:26, John 6:14, John 6:69, John 7:41, John 8:26, John 11:27, Acts 9:22, Acts 17:3, 1 John 5:1, Daniel 9:25

Mighty God (Isaiah 9:6)
Mighty One (Isaiah 60:16)
Morning star (Numbers 24:17, 2 Peter 1:19, Revelation 2:28, Revelation 22:16)

Nazarene (Matthew 2:23)

Only begotten Son (John 1:18, John 3:16)
Our Passover (1 Corinthians 5:7)

Perfect man (Isaiah 53:9, John 1:14, 2 Corinthians 5:21, Hebrews 5:9)
Prince of Kings (Revelation 1:5)
Prince of Life (Acts 3:15)
Prince of Peace (Isaiah 9:6)
Prophet (Deuteronomy 18:18, Matthew 21:11, Matthew 21:46, Mark 6:15, Luke 7:16, Luke 13:33, John 4:19, John 6:14, John 7:40, John 9:17, Acts 3:22)

Redeemer (Job 19:25)
Resurrection and Life (John 11:25)
Rock (Isaiah 8:14, Matthew 11:6, Matthew 13:57, Mark 6:3, Romans 9:32, 1 Corinthians 1:23, 1 Peter 2:8, 1 Corinthians 10:4)

Root of David (Revelation 22:16)
Rose of Sharon (Song of Solomon 2:1)
Savior (Luke 2:11)
Seed of woman (Genesis 3:15, Galatians 4:4)
Shepherd and Bishop of souls (1 Peter 2:25)
Shiloh (Genesis 49:10)

Son of the Blessed (Mark 14:61)
Son of David (Matthew 1:1)
Son of God (Matthew 2:15, 1 Chronicles 17:11–15)
Son of the Highest (Luke 1:32)
Son of Man (Matthew 8:20)
Sun of Righteousness (Malachi 4:2)
Star of Jacob (Numbers 24:17)
Sun (Psalm 19:4, Psalm 84:11)
Servant of the Lord (Isaiah 53:11)

True Light (John 1:9)
True Vine (John 15:1–27)
Truth (John 1:14)

Witness (Isaiah 55:4)
Word (John 1:1–4, 1 John 1:1, John 5:7, Revelation 19:13)
Water of Life (John 4:9–14)

"The words of a talebearer are as wounds, and they go down into the innermost parts of the bearer" (Proverbs 26:22).

Our words create our world.

"Where no wood is, there the fire goeth out: so where there is no talebearer, the strife ceaseth" (Proverbs 26:20).

"A word fitly spoken is like apples of gold in pictures of silver" (Proverbs 25:11).

"But I say unto you, That every idle word that man shall speak, they shall give account thereof in the day of judgment" (Matthew 12:36).

"For by thou words, thou shalt be justified, and by thou words thou shalt be condemned" (Matthew 12:37).

"Heavens and earth shall pass away, but my words shall not pass away" (Matthew 24:35).

"Then Simon Peter answered him, Lord, to whom shall we go? Thou hast the words of eternal life" (John 6:68).

"Let the word of Christ dwell in you richly in all wisdom, teaching and admonishing one another in psalms and hymns and spiritual songs, singing with grace in your hearts to the Lord" (Colossians 3:16).

"For our gospel came not unto you in word only, but also in power, and in the Holy Ghost, and in much assurance; as ye know what manner of men we were among you for your sake" (1 Thessalonians 1:5).

"Wherefore comfort one another with these words" (1 Thessalonians 4:18).

"Study to shew thyself approved unto God, a workman that needeth not to be ashamed, rightly dividing the word of truth" (2 Timothy 2:15).

"Preach the word; be instant in season, out of season, reprove, rebuke, exhort with all long suffering and doctrine" (2 Timothy 4:2).

"For the word of God is quick and powerful and sharper than any two edged sword, piercing even to the dividing asunder of soul and spirit, and of the joints and marrow, and is a discerner of the thoughts and intents of the heart" (Hebrews 4:12).

"But be ye doers of the word, and not hearers only, deceiving your own selves" (James 1:22).

"Being born again, not of corruptible seed, but of incorruptible, by the word of God, which liveth and abideth forever" (1 Peter 1:23).

"As newborn babes, desire the sincere milk of the word, that ye may grow thereby" (1 Peter 2:2).

"Likewise, ye wives, be in subjection to your own husbands, that, if any obey not the word, they also may without the word be won by the conversation of the wives" (1 Peter 3:1).

"That which was from the beginning, which we have heard, which we have seen with our eyes, which we have looked upon, and our hands have handled, of the Word of life" (1 John 1:1).

"But whoso keepeth his word, in him verily is the love of God perfected; hereby know we that we are in him" (1 John 2:5).

"My little children, let us not love in word, neither in tongue; but in deed and in truth" (1 John 3:18).

"And if any man shall take away from the words of the book of this prophecy, God shall take away his part out of the book of life, and out of the holy city, and from the things which are written in this book" (Revelation 22:19).

"Death and life are in the power of the tongue; and they that love it shall eat the fruit thereof" (Proverbs 18:21).

"The Lord bless thee, and keep thee. The Lord make his face shine upon thee, and be gracious unto thee. The Lord lift up his countenance upon thee, and give thee peace. And they shall put my name upon the children of Israel, and I will bless them" (Numbers 6:24–27).

CPSIA information can be obtained
at www.ICGtesting.com
Printed in the USA
BVHW041949240522
637949BV00004B/26